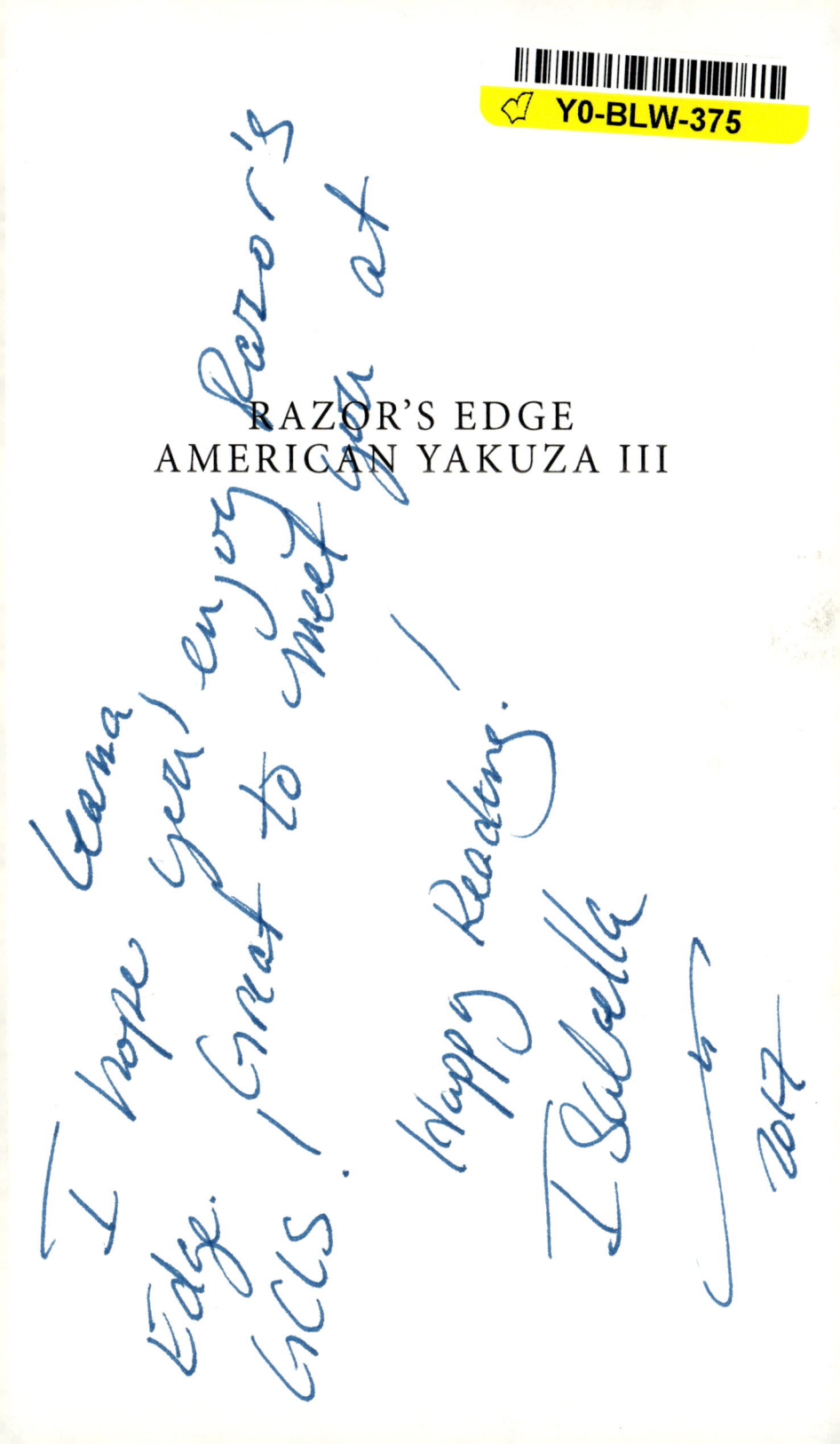

RAZOR'S EDGE
AMERICAN YAKUZA III

Liana,
I hope you enjoy Razor's Edge. Great to meet you at GCLS. Happy Reading.
I Sulcella
2017

RAZOR'S EDGE
AMERICAN YAKUZA III

ISABELLA

SAPPHIRE BOOKS

SALINAS, CALIFORNIA

Razor's Edge - American Yakuza III
Copyright © 2017 by Isabella All rights reserved.

ISBN -978-1-943353-81-1

This is a work of fiction - names, characters, places, and incidents are the product of the author's imagination or are used fictitiously. Any resemblance to actual persons living or dead, business, events or locales is entirely coincidental.

All rights reserved. No part of this publication may be reproduced, distributed, or transmitted in any form or by any means, including photocopying, recording, or other electronic or mechanical methods, without written permission of the publisher.

Editor - Shelley Thrasher
Book Design - LJ Reynolds
Cover Design - Michelle Brodeur

Sapphire Books Publishing, LLC
P.O. Box 8142
Salinas, CA 93912
www.sapphirebooks.com

Printed in the United States of America
First Edition –   April 2017

This and other Sapphire Books titles can be found at
www.sapphirebooks.com

Dedication

Mom

Acknowledgment

It is with great respect that I thank my editor. This book wouldn't be anything without, Shelley Thrasher.

Chapter One

Luce's head bobbed back, waking her from a sick, twisted nightmare where a Russian sadist cuffed and beat her. But it wasn't a dream.

She jerked her arms, which were twisted around the rungs of the chair she'd been intimate with the last couple of days. Her shoulders screamed in agony, frozen from being tied behind her back. She tried one more time to escape from the metal bracelets. The blood from her raw wrists coated her palms as she tried to push one side off and then the other.

No use. They were as tight today as they had been when Petrov placed them there. She just needed one minute to kill the bastard.

A slight draft wafted through the dark, dirty room. The smell of urine, blood, and her own sweat hovered around her the way warm fog on a humid Southern night levitated over the surface of a pond full of scum. She pushed her tongue against the nasty, bloody rag Petrov had shoved into her mouth when her wails of pain became too loud. When she'd spit it out and told him to go fuck himself, he'd slapped her, almost knocking her out, and tied the gag in place.

It wasn't as if the noisy neighbors were going to say anything. They'd fought a battle royal every night she'd been here. Bottles crashed against the walls, and sobbing women had lulled her to sleep, when she could sleep. She suspected she was in one of Petrov's whorehouses, judging by the constant yelling in Russian. Every once in a while she caught a Russian female voice, but other than that, she heard mostly men screaming and women crying.

She couldn't stand her own stench. What she wouldn't do for a shower. Her stomach cramped again. Great. Her period was coming. She couldn't cut a break, even if she had a dozen pairs of rusty scissors. Since they weren't giving her a shower, she doubted they'd provide any feminine products. *If they'd only open a window.*

Wasn't this rich? How could the head of one of the biggest crime families sit trussed up like a Christmas pig just waiting to be put out of her misery? She knew how. Her mind had been wrapped around a beautiful brunette who'd just fought the fight of her life and was just barely coming back from a vicious attack, thanks to that bastard Frank. The fog of revenge was edging further in on her thoughts, trying to shove out everything else, but she needed to stay focused on getting out of the room and saving her own life.

Luce pushed against the rag, hoping for just enough room to push down the bile threatening to spew. "What a way to go," she muttered. "I'll die drowning in my own puke."

Pulling in a staggered breath, she was sure she had at least one broken rib and probably a collapsed lung. The pain ebbed through her chest, each breath becoming shallower than the last. It felt like a knife was wedged between her ribs. That was the least of her worries as she looked down at the revolver and the single bullet that sat on the coffee table in front of her. Problem was, Luce doubted she'd survive another round of Russian roulette. Her number was bound to come up. She needed to devise a plan, fast.

For two days she'd taken a beating and now had a hard time making out anything in the room. Her reward for being stubborn. She refused to tell Petrov where his wife and daughter were—bargaining chips to get her hands on Frank—but maybe she should reconsider her options. She'd hoped Frank would be the one to eventually come in and mete out her punishment.

No luck, so far. Clearly Petrov was saving all the fun for himself.

"Luce." Petrov's voice boomed as the door slammed against the wall. "Jesus, it stinks in here."

She tried to follow him as he pranced around the room. Just two minutes. She just needed one hand free and two minutes. Then he wouldn't be strutting around like the cock of the walk. She envisioned her hand digging into his throat, his windpipe between her fingers and thumb. She could almost hear the soft, squishy bits popping as she squeezed, choking the life out of his sorry ass. She'd take pleasure watching him die in front of her. That's what kept her alive, that and Brooke. A pang of relief settled her. At least Brooke was somewhere safe and out of Petrov's reach.

"How is that sweet little sister of yours? Mei, right?" His broken English assaulted her ears. He'd made a point of trying to have a conversation with her each time he came in, but it was always one-sided. Her contempt for him kept her mouth locked shut. Responding to the arrogant prick would only spur him further, and she wanted this over, one way or the other.

Luce rolled her eyes and looked away, dismissing him.

"What's that?" Petrov said as he lowered his head close to her face. "God, you stink. What would Brooke say if she could see your filthy ass now?"

Luce turned her head toward him and blew her nose. A smattering of blood spattered on his face. Within an instant, a stinging slap snapped her head back. Her reward for the defiant gesture.

"I got to give it to you, Luce. You don't give up," he said, wiping his face. "I should put you in one of my whorehouses. With that body, those exotic looks, and that tenacity you would be a hit. Once you healed up, but then, you know? Funny thing about men. They like to beat on women, and well, we know you can take a punch. Ehh?"

"Uck you," she mumbled around the gag.

"Yes, yes. Petrov knows you want to fuck him, but honestly, you're not my type. Now where is my wife and daughter? Tell me and I make this quick, no spinning cylinder. I just put bullet..." He stuck his finger between her eyebrows. "Here, da?"

"Iss off."

"Ha, ha. Good for you. Tell you what. If you survive this round, which I doubt, I let you take a piss in the bathroom instead of that bucket." He pointed to the paint bucket in the corner responsible for much of the stench in the room.

Petrov picked up the revolver and made a dramatic show of swinging the cylinder open. He spun it.

Zip, zip, zip.

He pushed the single bullet into one of the chambers and slapped it closed. Short, shallow breaths kept pace with the tick, tick, tick of the cylinder as he spun it again.

Luce remembered the same exact scenario playing out in the past, but it was her father who sat on the business end of a revolver.

Luce could see the muscles working as JP clenched his jaw tight. He was going to be a pain in her ass until she dealt with him, and she now had her grandfather's permission to handle the issue he'd brought upon her family. As she looked down his chest, she caught a glimpse of chrome pop out from under his jacket. Reaching for the gun, she pulled a .357 revolver from a shoulder holster. She shot Sammy a look and shook her head. It pissed her off that he'd missed something so potentially dangerous. She would deal with that disappointment at another time. This time was reserved for a family reunion that wouldn't end well.

"You're such a fucking cowboy, JP. A chrome revolver. Really? How come I'm not surprised?"

Hefting the weight in her hand, she noted the pearl handles. Her father was never a practical man, from what she remembered, and his choice in guns confirmed he still had an even bigger ego. Pushing JP's head forward as she released her grip on it, she took a step back and turned the gun over in her hand. It was impractical, clunky, and more of a showpiece than a working piece of equipment. Nothing like the .380 she had strategically placed back in her waistband.

As she rolled the cylinder, the light reflected off the ridges of the spinning barrel. She pulled the catch and emptied the bullets from the gun. Luce made sure JP was watching as she slid a single bullet into one of the chambers. She made a show of closing the cylinder with the flick of her wrist. Hearing it lock, she spun the cylinder again. When it stopped, she looked at her father.

"So, tell me again why you're here, JP."

Pointing the business end at her father, she cocked her head, squinted her eyes, and waited. If he was scared, he didn't show any sign of it.

He looked down the barrel pointed at his forehead. "You wouldn't dare."

"Oh, but I would. Now, let's try this again. What are you doing here, and don't make me ask again."

Luce pulled the hammer back one click, feeling the hatch pattern on the hammer bite into her thumb. One more click back would make the gun ready to do what it was made to do, kill. Locking eyes with JP, she willed her stoic features not to change. In fact, she hardened her stare at the one man she hated more than Petrov.

"I wasn't doing anything. I was having a drink in a club, relaxing. I didn't know it was one of your grandfather's."

"It isn't one of his. It's one of mine, and I think you knew that, didn't you?"

"Since when do you have the money to own a club?"

"Since my grandfather made me oyabun. I own everything now, JP."

"Well, this changes things, now, doesn't it?"

"Not for me."

Another click of the hammer, and it was ready to do her bidding. She was in control of her father's life, and she liked the feeling. Her heart was beating so hard she could hear it pounding in her ears as the blood rushed through her body. She had waited for this moment for decades, and she wasn't about to be denied. Putting the barrel against his thigh, she moved close enough that her nose was almost touching his. She wanted him to look her in the eyes when he lied, again.

"Last time. Sure you don't want to change your

story?"

"You won't shoot me. I'm your father."

Luce looked at her genetic maker and smiled wickedly. She hated him more than anything on this earth, and here he was toying with the idea that he could play the "daddy" card. Could he actually believe that somehow, being his daughter, she would give him a pass for all the things he had said and done in her life? Oh, was he going to be disappointed. Luce pulled the trigger, and the empty pop echoed throughout the warehouse. It was his lucky day.

Karma was a bitch, wasn't it? Well, if she had her way she'd make it her bitch today.

The muzzle of the barrel pressed against her temple, just as it had every day for the past two days. She shifted, planted her feet firmly on the floor, stiffened, and sat up ramrod straight. She thought of her father as he looked straight at her, the barrel of his chrome deliverance pushed against his head.

"Just like you to go out like Yakuza."

"Uck you."

The click of the hammer being pulled back echoed through the room like a death knell. Looking straight ahead, she took a slow, deep breath and held it. The tension was so thick it was hanging like moss from a Southern oak. She could see Petrov was getting off on the dramatic display. A smile creased his greasy face.

Suddenly, it was as if someone had hit the slow-motion button on the world as she caught sight of Petrov's finger pulling the trigger.

Bang!

"God damn, you're one lucky bitch, Potter." Petrov laughed, slapping Luce on the back.

Her insides were jelly. And if she didn't know better, she thought she'd wet herself. She had dodged a bullet, literally, and time wasn't on her side. A cramp exploded through her body, doubling her over with a groan.

"Okay, okay, no need to be so dramatic, Luce." Petrov snapped the cylinder open, dropped the bullet into his palm, and looked at it. "Must be a magic bullet. Ha, ha." He shoved it in front of her face for a look, then placed it back on the table just as he'd done the past two days.

"Pee," Luce choked out, reminding him of his promise.

"Okay, okay. Petrov is man of his word. I'll send one of my guys in to take you wee wee." He said the last part of the sentence in a singsong, childlike voice.

"Mmm,"

"What?"

"Mmmm," she repeated.

He reached up and pulled the gag off, and she spit it out. "Pee now."

"Patience, Grasshopper." Petrov laughed uncontrollably at the reference.

"Fuck you," Luce said, defiance coloring her reply.

SWACK. Petrov backhanded Luce.

She tongued the broken lip, the coppery taste of blood coating her mouth. He reached down and squeezed her chin between his beefy hands, forcing her to look up at him.

"Do you kiss Brooke with that mouth? You really

should be nicer to your captors. I'm the only reason you're still alive. And I'm not finding myself able to put up with more bullshit."

Luce tried to avert her gaze. The sight of him made her want to puke on purpose.

He jerked her face back and forth. "Look at me when I'm talking to you, bitch." He held her face while he backhanded her again. His knuckles connected with her jaw, rattling her head. "I said, look at me."

Luce's eyes were so swollen she could barely see his face, but she could feel and smell his hot breath on her own face. Whatever he'd had for lunch wasn't agreeing with him.

"See. Two bosses can be civil to each other. Da?" He pinched her chin tight before releasing it and pushing it away from him. "You know, Luce, you're still beautiful woman. Perhaps we can come to agreement… you know…" She could feel his lips moving her hair over her ear as he spoke. "How do they say? Quid pro quo. You give me something. I give you something."

She wasn't giving this bastard anything, except maybe a knife in the gut. If he was lucky, she wouldn't twist as she jerked up on it and cut the fat bastard.

"You promised me I could go pee. Are you a man of your word or not?" Her voice sounded like gravel being rubbed together. She swallowed hard, but what little saliva she had burned as it went down.

Petrov sneered. "Petrov always man of his word." He stalked to the door, practically pulling it off its hinges as he opened it. After he yelled something in Russian, Luce heard chairs scraping against the floor and feet running in different directions. At least two other people were in the house, not good odds for someone in her condition.

"Someone will come to take you to the toilet."

With that, Petrov was gone and yelling more Russian. Luce had to come up with a plan, and quick. Otherwise she was sure the next time he raised a gun, he'd make sure she was dead. At least that's what she would do.

Chapter Two

Three days earlier

The unmistakable aroma of antiseptic and cleaning solution bit Luce's nostrils, waking her. Someone from housekeeping swished the mop around the floor. Without thinking, she pulled out her handkerchief and covered her nose, trying not to be too offensive to the woman who was just doing her job.

Luce hated hospitals. They only brought death, as far as she was concerned. The smells, the lights, and the nurses clad in scrubs all reminded her of her time spent with her dying grandfather. She'd kept a bedside vigil as he struggled to battle the aggressive cancer that finally claimed his life. He handled his pain as he handled all loss, especially that of his wife—taken in the prime of her life. Then the loss of his only daughter, Luce's mother. He had faced his impending death with dignity and honor, never complaining about the disease that had a stranglehold on his last breaths. She'd never forget the last sound as the nurse had pushed her out of his room. The flat-line beep had torn through her like a sharp tanto blade, forever scoring her soul.

Luce shaded her eyes as the flickering fluorescent lights played on her last nerve, just as they did every time they were flicked on. Nurses, unannounced, rushed in to take Brooke's vitals, and housekeeping dashed around the room to clean, avoiding Luce's penetrating gaze. The mop swerved under the bed, just missing Luce's loafers. She raised her feet as the swirling machine darted to where she'd just been taking up real estate, and then it was gone again, leaving behind the skid marks of acrid cleaning solution. They'd done this dance every day for the past week, and it always ended the same way. Backing out, the woman pulled the bucket backward, slung the curtain closed, and Luce ordered, "Lights."

The buzzing ended immediately, and Luce could go back to her vigil, this time watching Brooke breathe and knowing she would get out of the death chamber. Luce planted her chin back on the bed and watched Brooke sleep. Every once in a while she mumbled or moaned in pain, and like a working dog, Luce alerted, stood, and ran her fingers over Brooke's brow, trying to offer some comfort. Most times Brooke turned her head away from Luce's touch, but the few times she'd awoken, she offered Luce a meager smile, her eyes barely registering Luce's presence. Then she mumbled an apology as she faded back into her drug-induced fog.

It pained Luce to see Brooke so damaged, so broken. The stab wound to her side had almost been fatal. In the mix of panic and urgency that day, Luce had shattered every speed record and blown through most red lights as she raced to get her lover to the hospital. She'd watched Brooke, motionless in the backseat, with one eye and kept the other riveted on traffic. The only other thing she focused on was the revenge she would exact on Frank for nearly taking Brooke's life. She'd promised her grandfather only weeks earlier as he lay dying in this very hospital that Frank would pay. Now she was doubly sure it would be a slow, painful death, Yakuza style.

Luce rolled her head to the side so she could rest and still watch Brooke. She'd been there for hours already. A bedside watch was a small price to pay compared to what could have happened. Luce laced her fingers between Brooke's and brought the fragile digits to her lips, kissing each one. She'd survived the vicious attack at the hands of Frank, her grandfather's own Benedict Arnold. The second-in-command had defected to the Russians and was hell-bent on destroying Luce, her business, and everything she loved.

She couldn't even imagine her world without her lover, yet she'd almost had to. Her heart had hardened when she lost her grandfather. The loss of Tamiko had pushed her to the edge. But the attack on Brooke almost broke her. When she wasn't focused on Brooke, her thoughts of revenge comforted her most. She was relieved when Colby Water had informed her that the charges against her boss, Deputy Chapel, would stick. Luce hated the way the story had played out, but dirty DOJ officials were worse than crime bosses. You expected bosses to do whatever they could to get ahead, but a government official? Oh, that was criminal.

Luce rubbed her cheek against Brooke's knuckles, then turned her hand over and kissed Brooke's palm.

The soft crackle of Brooke's voice broke Luce's concentration. "How long have you been here, baby?"

"Hey. How are you feeling?" Luce smiled, stood, and kissed Brooke's forehead. "Are you thirsty?"

Brooke persisted. "How long?"

"Not long."

"Liar. You don't have to play nursemaid, honey." Brooke tapped her lips, and Luce complied. Delicately, she placed a soft kiss on Brooke's lips. Resting her forehead against Brooke's, she answered truthfully. "I'm going to be here every day until you get out."

"Honey," Brooke whispered. "You need to go back to work. They're taking good care of me. Don't worry."

But Luce did worry. Brooke hadn't healed as easily as the doctors hoped. She'd contracted a staph infection, and that added to the trauma her body was already fighting. They had to find another course of antibiotics, because the last one hadn't done the trick, so they'd hit her hard with stronger stuff. Even with all of Luce's money, she couldn't buy Brooke's health.

The doctors all said the same thing. "It's a marathon, not a race. So be prepared." She'd heard the comment so often that finally she told the doctors if they said it one more time, she couldn't be responsible for her actions.

"Luce?"

"Huh?"

"Go home." Brooke was trying to sound firm, her pale-bluish lips pressed into a thin, tight line.

"Stop," Luce said, patting Brooke's hand. Pulling the chair closer, she kissed her hands and smiled. "I'm not going anywhere. End of discussion."

Before she could say anything else, her phone buzzed. She ignored it and focused on Brooke.

"Are you going to get that? It could be important."

"No. I told Sammy and the guys not to call me under any circumstances, so it isn't business." The phone went dead. "See. It's not important."

Brooke put her cool hand on Luce's face, her thumbs running over Luce's top lip. "I love you."

"I love you, too," Luce said, then gently bit Brooke's thumb in a playful way.

"I want to start a family."

"What?" Luce asked around the thumb still in her mouth.

Brooke looked at her and hooked her thumb, pulling Luce's face closer to hers. "I want to have kids. I want something that grounds us."

Luce just sat there, stunned. Kids? They hadn't even talked marriage, yet. Not that Luce was opposed to marriage. Almost losing Brooke had solidified that longing. But family?

"Shouldn't we get married first?" Luce said as she pulled the thumb from her lips.

"Are you asking?"

"Of course, but not like this...I mean...well, this isn't how I wanted to propose. Besides, we need to get you well, back on your feet."

Luce stood and smoothed her button-down, tucking the tails of her shirt back into her slacks.

"I'm not saying right away, Luce. But someday"

"Oh, right. Okay, sure. Someday."

Luce's phone buzzed again. Without thinking, she pulled it and recognized the number. Poking the face, she sent it to voicemail, then cursed herself for even looking. Brooke's request for kids had caught her off guard, discombobulated her world.

A parent?

Her?

Was she ready for that kind of responsibility? Her phone went off again, and once more, she looked at it without thinking. Sammy was persistent. He was also going to pay for his determination.

"You should probably get that. It must be important if they keep calling," Brooke insisted.

"It's just Sammy. He knows better. I gave him

strict—"

"Then it is important. He wouldn't risk your wrath unless something needed your attention."

Brooke was right. Sammy knew better than to disregard her. Looking at Brooke, she nodded and pointed to the door. "I'll take it in the hallway."

"You don't have to go outside. I'm awake."

"Right," Luce said, sitting down. Adjusting herself in the chair she had been intimate with over the past few weeks, Luce turned her head away from Brooke and whispered, "This better be life-or-death, Sammy."

"Boss, I'm sorry to bother you, but you got a delivery."

"That's not life-or-death, Sammy."

"Hmm—"

"Stick it in my office, and when I get there I'll open it."

"Well, I don't think I can put it in your office."

Now Luce was getting agitated. "Okay, take the fucking package to my house, and when I get home tonight, I'll deal with it."

"Uhm, Boss. I think you better come to the office. Now."

Luce stood and stepped out into the hallway so Brooke couldn't hear her yelling. "What the fuck is wrong with you, Sammy? Put the fucking package in—"

"Boss, it's a woman."

"What's a woman?"

"The package. It's a woman, and she says she needs to deliver a message to you. Says she's supposed to give it only to you."

"You've got to be kidding me."

"No, I wish I was, but I think you need to get over here, now. I can't explain it to you. You'll have to see it with your own eyes."

The hair on Luce's neck stood on end. Sammy sounded strange. He never got frustrated or scared, and he sure didn't call her about a situation when he could handle it himself. In fact, he rarely called her to handle a situation. That's why he was her second-in-command. She didn't have to micro-manage him, and he never let her down.

"Are you on speaker?"

"No."

"Okay, is someone forcing you to call me? You okay?"

"Boss, I just think you need to get over here. You know, I wouldn't call if it wasn't…"

Luce pressed him. "If it wasn't what?"

"I can't explain it, Boss."

"Don't move. I'm on my way."

"Please tell Ms. Erickson I'm sorry."

Luce didn't reply. She cut him off and stuffed the phone into her pocket as she whispered, "This better be fucking important."

Chapter Three

"Everything all right?" Brooke whispered as she smoothed the veins on the back of Luce's hand. Luce had been hovering ever since the attack. While she loved her girlfriend with all her heart, Luce was wearing a path in the cement of her kennel, acting like a pent-up pit bull with too much energy. It was starting to wear on her, too. "Honey, why don't you find out what's going on?"

Brooke tried to turn on her side to face Luce, but the knife wound she'd suffered seemed to pull no matter how she moved. Frank had almost taken her life, and all she could see on Luce's face was revenge when the subject came up. Her ex, Colby Water, had come by to visit and give Luce some information on the status of the case against Luce. Whatever they'd talked about had gone right over Brooke's head. The painkillers had made the last week an absolute blur, and justifiably so, the doctor had said when she complained. She needed to rest to recuperate. Now, if her body would just hurry things up.

When she was awake, she'd had lots of time to think. Her mind wandered to the what-ifs and what-could-have-beens, and all she knew was that she was thinking about long-term things, like marriage and kids. Brooke wasn't certain Luce was on the same track as she was, but she wanted to find out. Sending out the first trial balloon had told her what she'd expected—

Luce wasn't quite ready, yet.

"Sweetheart?" Luce bent down and lay on the bed face-to-face with Brooke. "You okay?"

Brooke offered a slight smile. "Yeah. I'm good." She reached up and ran her fingers along Luce's cheek and then her lips. She caressed the slight bow of her top lip and then let her finger slip inside her mouth. "I love you."

Luce bit the tip of Brooke's finger, spearing her to her core.

Talking around her arousal, Luce smiled and said, "You're going to make me forget you're in a hospital."

"Is that the only thing you ever think of?"

"Honestly? Maybe."

"That's my dragon." Brooke pinched her chin and pulled Luce's lips closer. Without further words, Brooke allowed Luce to roll her to her back and let her passion flair. Maybe that would help fire off some loose nervous energy. Before things could move any further, Luce's phone went off again, the moment lost. At least for Brooke.

"You better get that." She pulled back and smiled at her ardent lover.

"Grrr." Luce pulled out the phone, looked at the screen, and then tucked it back into her jacket. "I better go. Sammy's not going to give up."

"I don't know what's going on, but promise me you'll be careful."

Luce picked up Brooke's hand and kissed the back of it, then turned it over and kissed her palm. "I'll tell you everything when I get back. I promise. No more keeping you in the dark."

Brooke didn't plan to make Luce keep that promise. Her business was sealed in secrecy, and it was probably better if she wasn't a part of that side of Luce's life. It had almost cost her her own life. However, it was her own fault. If she'd listened to Luce, she probably wouldn't have been stabbed or watched Lynn die right in front of her.

She'd never forget seeing her bodyguard Lynn dead, lying in a pool of her own blood. Her vacant eyes still haunted Brooke's dreams. In fact, she relived the whole day repeatedly, wishing the outcome had been different. But she couldn't will a different set of circumstances for them all. She would carry this scar for the rest of her life, like the one she wore. It would never leave her.

"You don't have to tell me anything, honey. Your business is your business."

"No. That's what got us into this situation in the beginning. I pushed you away, thinking it was for your own good. But it only created an opening for someone to capitalize on, and look at the damage it caused, the lives that were lost. I'll never forgive myself for what happened to you and Lynn." Luce ducked her head and rubbed Brooke's knuckles against the side of her face. "Ever," she whispered.

"Give it time, sweetheart. Give it time. Now go. Sammy's waiting."

The gentleness with which Luce kissed her sent a shiver through Brooke. At least some things were starting to get back to normal.

"We should find out when you're getting sprung from this place."

"Not soon enough for me." Brooke smiled and then motioned with her hands. "Shoo."

"I'll see you in a few hours."

"Go." Brooke made an attempt to shove Luce off

her and toward the door, but her body was immovable.

"Are you that ready to get rid of me?" Luce was joking.

"No, my love, but the sooner you go and see what's wrong with Sammy, the sooner you can fix the problem and come back."

"Hmm." Luce's forehead creased with doubt.

"I'll see you later."

Without another word, Luce turned to leave.

"Can you turn off the lights, please?"

Luce looked back at Brooke and winked. "What did you have in mind?"

"Sleep," she said flatly.

"Oh." Hitting the lights, Luce said softly, "I love you."

"I love you, too."

Brooke wondered how her life had come to this. A simple reporter who was now the lover of a Yakuza crime boss. Now, the question was, would she finally be able to control that little dragon Luce carried around?

※※※※※

Luce pushed her SUV through the city. The quicker she handled the issue at the office, the quicker she could get back to Brooke. As for the Russian, well, his daughter still worked for Luce, and eventually he'd want to see her. When he did, Luce would be ready. She wasn't a prisoner. Just the opposite. She could leave any time she wanted. Luce hoped she would, and when she did, Luce anticipated that she would lead them right to Petrov.

Luce pulled into her spot in front of Potter Enterprises and could see Sammy pacing, waiting for her. He stabbed the cigarette into the hot concrete and then picked up the butt.

"Boss, I'm so sorry, but she says she isn't leaving. She has a message for you, and she says only she can give it to you. Said her life depended on it and—"

Luce put her hand up. "Sammy."

"Yes, Boss."

"Did you get Lynn's family taken care of?"

Lynn's death had hit Luce hard. Knowing Frank had killed her made it even tougher. She hadn't spilled all the details of Lynn's death when she visited Lynn's parents. When they asked why, Luce had only one answer: she died in the service of another. The stoic face of Lynn's mother was the epitome of Japanese culture. She simply looked at Luce, closed her eyes, and bowed. She took her leave as Luce discussed the funeral arrangements and the money they would receive to compensate for the loss of their daughter. They knew the life of the Yakuza could be short, but to Luce, Lynn's death was unacceptable.

Turf wars weren't exactly uncommon for Luce and her business, so being at war with the Russian was the cost of doing business. Except he trafficked in drugs and flesh, and she didn't allow that type of trade in her territory. Clearly Petrov didn't like rules, but he liked battle, and it was clear one was raging between her and Petrov. Frank would be enemy number one in that war, and he was going down first. Whatever advantage Petrov thought he had by having Frank around would soon be a liability.

"Yes, Oyabun." Sammy bowed, then quickly opened the huge dragon door.

"I want you to personally visit her parents once a month and present them with the check."

"Yes, Oyabun."

"Now, tell me what the hell is going on in my office." Luce pressed the elevator button, pulled off her long black coat, and slung it over her arm. Pulling her arm in tight, she could feel the Beretta Nano just under her armpit. It gave her a sense of reassurance, tucked away in the nylon tank-top concealer. She'd started carrying her gun again, having become a bit lax just before the attack on Brooke, but that would never happen again.

"Who's in my office, Sammy?"

"Oyabun, if I told you, you wouldn't believe me. So you'll just have to see it for yourself."

"Who's in there with her?"

"Momo and Ms. Wentworth." Momo had replaced Lynn and moved up in the family ranks when Frank had killed her second, who was protecting Brooke. He'd regarded his position with the same intensity as Lynn had when she was in Luce's inner circle.

"Who's with Kat?"

Petrov's daughter, Kat, was Luce's bargaining chip, and she wasn't about to lose the one thing Petrov valued almost as much as money. He'd tried to plant Katerina in the club, trying to make Luce think she had simply applied for a job in Luce's new VIP club. The dancers she was hiring were actually designed to pump the VIPs for information on their business dealings, especially dealings Luce had a particular interest in. That had been Petrov's first mistake. He had underestimated Luce's connections and overestimated her libido. Luce had allowed Kat to stay on, in trade, and Luce kept her protected. More importantly, she was up a pawn in the chess game between her and

Petrov.

"Sasha's with Kat."

"Seriously?" Luce gave him a cold stare.

"She volunteered," he said, nervously poking the button repeatedly. Sasha said she was bisexual; however, she knew Lynn and Sasha had been lovers. It had practically killed Sasha when Luce broke the news of Lynn's murder. Sasha went into a rage that took days to work itself out of her system. Then, well, Luce still didn't know what to expect from her number three. So she gave Sasha space. Now it sounded like she was after some catnip. At the moment, she was the least of Luce's problems.

"Did you check our guest for any weapons?"

"Of course," Sammy said, holding the elevator door for Luce. "How is Ms. Erickson, Oyabun?"

Luce knew Sammy felt responsible for the attack on Brooke. She and Sammy had formed a connection after Sammy saved her from the two Russians who tried to carjack her. He had taken the call when Luce had refused to answer. She thought she was distancing Brooke from herself, protecting her. Instead, she'd practically put Brooke right in their hands.

"She's getting better," Luce said, clasping Sammy on the shoulder and squeezing.

That was as demonstrative as Luce would ever get with her family. She kept her emotions on a tight leash, especially after what had happened to Brooke and Lynn.

The elevator stopped and puked them out on Luce's office floor. The hum of the office stopped the moment someone caught sight of Luce. She hadn't been there in weeks, so she suspected everyone would be craning their necks and stop whatever they were doing the minute she arrived.

"Ms. Potter, it's good to see you back," Allie Wentworth, her assistant, said, making quick strides to keep up with her.

"Ms. Wentworth," Luce said curtly.

"Shall I bring tea?"

"Have you offered any to our guest?"

Allie looked at Sammy and then back at Luce before answering. "No, ma'am. I was told not to go in."

Luce walked past her assistant. "I see." Then she turned toward Sammy and shot him a sideways glance. She placed her jacket on Allie's desk and looked over at Sammy. "Then yes, please bring in tea and those cookies I like."

Stopping in front of her door, she tossed a request over her shoulder. "And have a dozen red roses sent to Brooke."

"Yes, ma'am, and you want the card to read…"

"No card needed."

Luce slammed the door behind her, leaving Sammy and Allie staring at each other. The door opened briefly again and spit out Momo.

"Oh, shit," he said, straightening his tie and coat.

Chapter Four

Luce let her gaze wander around the room, making sure the woman hadn't pilfered any of the small artwork that dotted the shelves and desk. Suddenly, the room looked different to her. She hadn't been in her office for any length of time, but something felt off. The importance of any business that took place here didn't seem to matter at the moment. Well, at least while Brooke was still in the hospital. Perhaps that would change as soon as Brooke was released and on her way to feeling better, but after losing both her grandfather and snatching her lover from the jaws of an impending death, something had changed within her. She couldn't quite put her finger on it, but she didn't have the time to psychoanalyze herself at the moment.

Ms. Wentworth's delicate hand had kept the dust at bay, and her to-be-done pile had miraculously minimized itself.

Finally, Luce settled her stern glare on the woman sitting on her tweed couch, which dwarfed her small, fragile frame, practically sucking her down into its grasp. She sat ramrod straight, as if her own body was constraining her, eyes forward, without as much as a glance at Luce. Luce swallowed hard, as the woman was an exact replica of a younger Luce. She had short, spiky blond hair and gaunt features, but her almond-shaped, jade-green eyes were the clincher. Composing herself quickly, Luce could only stare for a moment before she gathered her wits.

"I understand you wanted to see me, Ms..." Luce crossed her arms and leaned against her desk, the edge biting her in the ass. She finally softened her look at the intruder.

A soft whisper forced its way across the room. "Potter."

"Is this a joke?"

"I don't believe so," the woman said. Her accent was undeniably Japanese. Her demure, understated mannerisms and her refusal to look Luce in the eye only solidified what Luce was thinking.

"Okay, so who sent you?"

What came out of her mouth next sent Luce into a tailspin. "Our father."

"My father is dead. Would you try again?"

"I believe you are mistaken."

"What's going on here?" Luce studied the woman. Somebody was up to something, and Luce was sure she was being played. "I don't have time for games."

"I was told to deliver a message to you upon my arrival in America."

"Who sent you? Frank?"

The fragile woman lowered her eyes at the thunderous sound of Luce's voice. "I was told if I did not deliver the message, I would be killed." Her voice was barely a whisper now.

She began to unbutton her blue silk jacket, but Luce stopped her. "Look, I don't know what kind of game you're playing, but deliver your message and then leave."

The woman didn't stop disrobing. She stood and turned away from Luce. Without hesitation Luce pulled her Beretta and aimed it at the woman, who was now naked from the waist up. In her younger days Luce might've enjoyed the sight of a nearly disrobed woman. However, she'd put those days and that life behind her, for Brooke.

Neither of them moved. Luce gasped, lowered her gun, and stared at the tattoo on the woman's back.

"Jesus Christ."

※ ※ ※ ※

"Hey, kid. How you doin'?"

Brooke roused herself from the sleep-induced fog that accompanied the oxycodone the doctors were giving her for the pain that never seemed to ease. On one hand, the haze was welcome. The drugs kept her from falling into those nightmares that kept invading the darkness, but they also seemed to keep her weak and immobile. On the downside, she didn't have the energy to get up to even go to the bathroom.

Expecting to see the doctor, instead she made out Colby Water standing at the end of the bed. She knew Luce had placed at least one person to stand guard outside her door, and that made her feel cared for, but how did Colby get past Luce's guard dogs?

"Hey...what are you doing here?"

"Well, I sorta expected to see Luce."

"You just missed her. She got a call and had to jet to the office."

Colby pulled the chair away from her bed and sat down. "Mind if I sit?"

"Aren't you already?"

"Good point. How are you?"

"I've had better months." Brooke's eyelids

weighed a thousand tons, and she struggled to keep them open. "What do you need with Luce? She's not in trouble, is she?" She slurred her words.

"No, no, nothing like that. I've just got some intel I wanted to share with her." Colby reached over and touched Brooke's hand. Her face took on a gentle look, and sad eyes met Brooke's. "I'm so sorry all of this happened to you, Brookie."

"It wasn't your fault, Colby."

Brooke felt bad for Colby. They'd been lovers years ago, and she'd come down hard on Brooke when she found out Luce and she were involved. To say Colby had read her the riot act would be like calling the riots at a Trump rally a small get-together. Brooke wouldn't call Luce and Colby friends, but they were mutually inclusive for the purposes of catching Petrov and Frank. Like one hand washing the other, they needed each other.

"I shouldn't have given you a bad time. I should have trusted Luce, but..." Colby looked down at their joined hands. "I...let my feelings for you get in the way of doing the right thing. I'm sorry."

Brooke, uncomfortable with the juxtaposition, patted Colby's hand. "It's all right."

"It's not, so please don't say that for my benefit. I screwed up and trusted the wrong person, and that person turned out to be dirty."

"Deputy Chapel was dirty?" Brooke hadn't been told about any of the circumstances surrounding her kidnapping and stabbing. She just thought Frank had gone rogue and come after her to get at Luce. Waking up tied to the chair in the warehouse with Petrov standing over her, threatening to kill her, was the first time she'd known Petrov was involved.

She could tell by the way Colby avoided her gaze that her words rang true. Brooke patted Colby's hand. It was her turn to be supportive. "You had no way of knowing, Col."

"I should have at least listened with half an ear to what Luce was telling me and then checked her facts. Instead, Chapel sent me on some wild goose chase. It's my own fault. I trusted my own command structure, and it almost cost you your life. I'm sorry for that, Brookie. Can you forgive me?"

"Colby, stop. Please. There was no way for you to know. You just saw Luce as this Yakuza crime head and went with your gut."

"That's just it. I didn't go with my gut. I went with my jealousy over Luce. She had someone I loved, and I couldn't understand what you saw in her."

Shocked, Brooke focused on Colby's mouth, trying to figure out if she was dreaming or lucid. She hoped this was a dream, because Brooke had never met this version of Colby Water. If she had, perhaps they'd be together today. Hmm, scratch that. Brooke hadn't been able to handle her womanizing. The arrogant, self-assured Colby was fine.

"Col, you just don't know her like I do. She's…" Brooke tried to find the right words to describe her lover without sounding too clichéd. "She's honest, has a code of ethics you wouldn't believe, adores her family, and would do anything for them. For Luce, family consists of the ones you pick, not those you're born with. JP was an example of her not being able to cut off a branch in the family tree."

"Did she kill him?" The question came out of thin air and floated out there.

Brooke wasn't about to confirm anything for

Colby. Besides, Luce had never told her what she'd done to JP, only that he was no longer going to be a problem for Luce or them. She'd explained in a cold, emotionless voice that Frank was next, even if it took her to her last breath to catch him.

"I don't know, Colby. What does it matter?"

Brooke's defensive tone should have told Colby to back off, but she didn't.

"I'm just wondering, Brookie. It's not a judgment call. Besides, she helped expose a dirty officer in the DOJ." Colby gazed down at her hands and fidgeted. "I'm sorry. I should never have asked."

This was that side of Luce's business that Brooke had said she didn't need to know about. Now she was sure she didn't want to pry. Some things were better left unsaid.

***

Sammy and Momo burst through the doors, guns drawn. "Boss."

"Get out," Luce screamed and pointed at the door. "Now."

"But Boss," Sammy said, staring at the woman.

"Get. Out." Luce pushed Sammy backward. "I'll call you if I need you."

Bowing and backing out of the door, Luce kicked it with her heel and slammed it shut. Turning back toward the woman, she noticed that her hands were clasped in front of her, her head bowed. She hadn't moved.

The tattoo stood out against the porcelain skin. A jade dragon similar to the one on Luce's front doors was etched on the woman's back. Red eyes, the color of fire, popped out as if looking directly at Luce. In its talons, it held an open scroll with Hangul writing stretched down in individual rows. Luce wished she had paid attention in her Korean language classes. Now she had nobody but herself to blame for not being able to read what was clearly meant for her on the scroll.

As Luce studied the tattoo, she could only marvel at the intricate artwork displayed in front of her. Luce had an appreciation for fine art, and this was a tattoo of the highest caliber. But what caught her attention most was at the bottom of the scroll: the initials JP, John Potter.

Chapter Five

"Who are you?"

"Mei Potter, a simple messenger."

"I don't understand."

"I was told that I am the messenger. I was to find you and deliver this message. If I did not succeed, I was to kill myself."

"What?" Luce touched the bare back. The ink wasn't fresh. "How long have you had this tattoo?"

"For many years," she whispered, her head still lowered. She stood dutifully as Luce traced the lines of the dragon with her fingers. Moving closer, she tried to read the Hangul but floundered. Her mind raced as she tried to force herself to remember her lessons. Something was different about these letters. They were Korean.

"I was told you might not believe me, so I was told what to say, Kaida."

Luce froze. Only her grandfather called her Little Dragon, and only one other person alive knew her nickname. Frank.

"Please don't be angry with me, sister."

Luce pulled her phone from her pocket and snapped several pictures. "Put your clothes back on," she directed the woman.

A soft knock pulled Luce's attention. "Come in."

"I have your tea, Ms. Potter." Allie peeked her head around the door.

"Put it on the table, Ms. Wentworth."

"Yes, ma'am."

Luce caught Allie's expression as the woman turned around, still buttoning her jacket.

"Not a word, Miss Wentworth. Understood?"

Luce's implication was clear. She wouldn't tolerate any office gossip.

"Of course, Ms. Potter."

Luce knew she didn't need to warn her. Allie had worked for Luce personally at her home, but it didn't hurt to remind her.

Luce waited until Allie left before she said anything else. "Please, sit down."

Luce pointed to the sofa and sat in the chair opposite her guest. She poured two cups of tea and motioned for the woman to take one. She cradled hers and stared into the dark liquid, trying to wrap her mind around what she'd seen. She was suspicious yet confused.

"What is your first name again?" Luce said as she blew on her tea before taking a sip.

"Mei."

"Mei." Luce looked at her mirror image. "And what is your last name, Mei?"

"Potter."

Luce put her thumb between her eyebrows and pressed, trying to alleviate the headache that was threatening to start.

"That's impossible, Mei. John Potter is dead. I killed him," Luce said, feeling no emotion for her sperm donor. She thought about the way he'd died, and her blood ran cold. She played that day out in her head.

As she pulled the hammer back once, she heard

the click echo through the room. The second click caused JP's eyes to widen. His brow furrowed as he challenged his daughter.

Luce chuckled. Clearly he didn't know her anymore. That was to her advantage.

"I hate to disappoint you, but—"

Her father screamed as the bullet passed through his thigh. The smell of cordite filtered up and scorched her nose, making her eyes water.

"You being my father means nothing to me."

Luce stepped back while JP stomped his leg, trying to do something about the pain. Tears rolled down his cheeks. He clamped his mouth shut, pressing his lips tight as if somehow it would lessen the pain. JP glared at her. Anger rolled off him, and he tensed against the waves of pain that had to be spreading through his rigid body.

"Let's try this once more." She dropped the empty casing from the cylinder, replaced it with another bullet, and spun the cylinder again. Luce pressed the warm tip of the barrel against his other thigh.

"What were you doing in my club?"

Their gazes locked, his challenging, hers questioning. She notched the hammer back one click and waited. JP's breathing was labored. He gasped when Luce moved her face closer to his. Arching an eyebrow, she eased the hammer back to its final resting place, ready to be deployed again. JP closed his eyes and waited, his lips sealed tight to suppress the scream on the verge of release.

"Nothing?"

Luce looked over at the three standing behind her. Their dispassionate faces were fixed on hers as she looked at one and nodded toward the table.

"Grab that rag and put it over his mouth. You." She pointed to another of her underlings. "Close the door and make sure no one's accidentally wandered into the warehouse to investigate, just in case Lynn or Sasha missed them."

Sammy stood silently by, awaiting his orders. His hands trembled, giving away his fear. Luce knew he was worried this might blow back on him again. Poor fellow. She sighed. She would have to meet with him to put him back on track with the organization. Accidents happened. That's why they were called accidents, but in her organization, they cost people their lives.

Focusing on her father again, she pushed the nozzle of the barrel harder into his leg.

"Last chance, Father."

He closed his eyes, a signal that he refused to give her what she wanted. This time when she pulled the trigger, his leg jerked as the bullet went through his thigh and out his heel. The agonized screams into the towel were slightly audible, but the man holding the towel pushed tighter on JP's mouth.

"Take it off. Let him breathe," Luce said, casually opening the cylinder and dumping the spent cartridge into her hand.

Inserting the four remaining bullets into the cylinder, she could smell the coppery odor of blood and cordite mixing, filling the room. She steeled herself for what was about to come. She owed her father nothing. The fact that he had contributed to her biology was a footnote on the long list of things she and her mother had been forced to endure at his hand while they were a family. Some things couldn't be forgotten or forgiven, not by Luce. Remembering how at peace her mother looked as she lay in her mahogany casket buffered any *feeling of empathy she might have for her father. No matter what she did, he would always be with her. She would never be able to forget him because every time she looked in the mirror, his eyes would stare back at her.* Blood pooled at JP's feet. She stepped back and ordered his legs wrapped with tourniquets. They would minimize the mess that the cleaning team would have to take care of later. The pallor of death covered JP's face. A gray tone replaced his normally pale coloring. His head flew forward as he passed out from the shock of being shot.

"Nuh-huh. You don't get off that easy, you bastard. Wakey, wakey. I want you to experience everything, Daddy. Like Mom did when you hung her."

Luce slapped his face to make him come around and ordered Sammy to bring her some water. As she poured it over his head, he pulled up, gasping as he breathed in the liquid.

"Good. Now are you taking me serious? Or would you like another example?"

"I told you—"

"Stop." Luce slapped his face. A handprint appeared on his cheek as the water enhanced the sting of the slap. She was losing patience with JP, and if he didn't know it yet, he soon would. She jerked back on his hair and bent to whisper in his ear. "Listen to me. I know you're working with Petrov. In fact, I know you bragged about being able to deliver me, dead or alive. Now, the question is, how do I deliver you to him—dead or alive?"

After she released his head, it slumped forward, his chin practically hitting his chest as it bounced. A maniacal laugh bubbled up from him, confusing Luce. Had he lost his mind, or was the pain so great that it clouded his judgment? Tossing his head back, he roared in laughter. "You are so fucking screwed, and you don't even know it. You played right into our hands."

"What're you talking about?" Luce stayed calm.

She had seen JP try to weasel his way out of things through lying, so she wasn't playing along this time. Waiting, she absentmindedly rolled the cylinder on the revolver, and the click echoed through the office. The muscles between her shoulders bunched together as tension filled her. JP continued to laugh. She slammed the butt of the gun in his face, making him pause before shooting her a dirty look. Luce smiled at his filthy, tear-soaked face. After tonight she would never see it again.

"Hmm, the way I see it, the only one screwed is you, JP. You have two holes..." Looking down at his legs, she corrected herself.

"Make those three holes in your legs, and the night isn't even over. So, if you even think you have any leverage here, you might want to reconsider your options."

"You're a little girl playing in a man's world, Luce. You have no idea what you've gotten yourself into, do you?"

"God, you are so dramatic, JP."

Rolling the cylinder, she placed it against his temple and pulled the hammer back one click. Taking a deep breath, she steeled herself against the rage building deep inside, trying as hard as she could to temper it with patience, but it was no use. She closed her eyes and saw her mother's beautiful face. Her soft, almond-shaped eyes seemed to close more when she smiled. Luce would often giggle and ask her mother if she could still see her when she smiled. Her mother's response was, "Of course, Kaida. You are always in my mind." Then she would bend down, cup her face, and kiss each of her pudgy cheeks.

How she missed her mother, and thanks to the bastard sitting in front of her, taunting her, she would never see her again, never kiss her good night, never feel herself wrapped in a warm, loving hug, ever. Her life had been replaced with the cold, hard reality that letting someone in might get them killed. So, she had adjusted her life accordingly. It was all his fault, and she owed him nothing but her hatred. She felt tears threaten but swallowed her pain. She would be damned if he would see her cry; he didn't deserve that pleasure.

"Any last words?" The cold, dead tone in her voice made JP turn and look at her.

If he thought he would find hope in her eyes, he was wrong.

"Wait."

"You have no lifelines, no friends to call, no one to help you, JP."

"Really?" He gasped. "What about that little reporter you're seeing, or your grandfather? Did you think I would be without options, Luce?"

"What're you talking about, old man? You have nothing to bargain with." Luce pressed the barrel harder into his temple.

"You really didn't think I'd come alone, did you?"

"Don't try to bullshit me. You don't have friends, JP, and it doesn't matter. You're going to die for what you did to my mother."

"Maybe you should listen to me for once, Luce. It could cost you dearly."

Looking down at her watch, she said, "You have five minutes." Luce tossed the revolver onto the table and took out her .380. She aimed it at JP. "Tick, tock, *asshole."*

JP had sat there so smug, even as he was bleeding out. God, she hated him. Those last few final moments were etched in her mind. His eyes, jade green. Now Mei carried those same genetics. Hadn't JP spread enough of his DNA around? What else was lurking around the corner, a son? A male assassin trained to take Luce's life as she'd taken JP's? She felt pulled back to the final minutes of JP's life. She hadn't thought of it in over a year, but here she was meandering through the nightmare of his existence once again.

Luce clapped her hands and rushed through the office to her father's limp form. Pulling out a pocketknife, she quickly sliced the bindings that held him, catching him as he pitched forward. Standing up with him, she suddenly felt him reach behind her, for her gun. As she wrestled with JP, she grabbed his thigh and squeezed as hard as she could. He let out a piercing scream, so close to her ear that she tossed a shoulder into his chest, forcing him back into the chair.

"You stupid bastard. You couldn't stop, could you?"

"Fuck you."

"You couldn't be a good guy for once, could you? Sammy, take care of him."

"You got it, Kaida."

"Why do you need one of your flunkies to do your dirty work?"

Luce turned toward her father and shook her head. He had to push her all the way, until the end, didn't he? Lifting the revolver, she pointed it at JP and pulled the trigger. "No. I can take out the trash."

The sound of gunfire made Luce duck. Someone was shooting at them from the warehouse floor, and she had a pretty good idea who it was. A bullet broke a glass window and hit JP in the back, spilling him to the floor.

He had died that night, hadn't he? Luce had to wonder. She remembered his body pitching forward past her to the floor. Then all hell broke loose, and everyone scattered like cockroaches when the lights were turned on. Now she wondered what had happened to her father's body.

"Ms. Potter? May I leave now? I have given you the message as instructed."

"No. I..." Luce wasn't about to let the woman go yet. Things weren't adding up, and she didn't know what the writing meant. A message from JP? His initials were at the bottom of that scroll.

"Keep your enemies close, Kaida," her grandfather had told her many times, so she wasn't about to let Mei Potter leave so quickly.

"Where are you staying?"

Mei looked up from her tea with a puzzled expression. "Why?"

"What were you told to do once the message was delivered?"

"I was instructed to wait at my hotel. Someone would pick me up."

"And take you where?"

"I don't know. I was just told to wait."

"Keep your enemies close, Kaida." Her grandfather's warning echoed in her mind.

Luce needed some space and time to think about what had just happened. No way was she going to let Mei out of her sight. Sammy was under strict orders not to let her leave. In fact, the only respectable thing was to offer to have Mei stay at her home. She wasn't ready to break the news to Brooke, yet. It would only complicate an already screwed-up situation. Shit, how was she going to deal with the possible reality that she had a sister, let alone explain it to Brooke? Luce was trying to emotionally detach herself from possibly having a sister or, worse, that her father, JP, could be alive. She needed to think about this situation logically. Who wanted Luce to be controlled by this sudden news?

Maybe it was time to pay a visit to her auntie and see if she knew anything. At least she could read the Hangul on the tattoo.

Yet her first priority was Brooke. That's where she needed to be right now. She wouldn't be out of the hospital for a few days. Enough time to question Mei further and do some background work on her long-lost sibling. Frank was behind this, she knew it. She just didn't know where all the lines were connected and who was pulling the ends. The thought that JP had orchestrated this sometime in the past, just to get revenge, was ludicrous, even for him. However, Luce wouldn't put it past her dearly departed father to have cooked up something with Frank and Petrov for revenge.

She thought about the logistics of a tattoo and its permanence, its meaning, and then finding someone willing to wear the ink for the rest of her life. It would take a large sum of money, but it could be done—assuming Mei was lying about her lineage. Contact lenses, a platinum dye job, and you'd have a close facsimile that could pass for Luce's sister.

God knew it must give Sammy and Momo the heebie-jeebies seeing her. Luce had to be honest. The girl was a walking image of her. So where should she start? She needed to prove the woman was a fraud. A DNA test was a good first step, assuming Mei agreed. If she didn't submit willingly, there were other ways to get her DNA. Luce hoped she didn't have to use any persuasive force.

Instead she'd call the one man who might be able to help her with the tattoo. He'd be able to tell her what she needed to know. A detour before the hospital was in order.

Chapter Six

Luce pushed the glass door of the inconspicuous tattoo shop open. If the average person didn't know about it, they would never suspect they had one in their upscale little shopping mall. It didn't come with the requisite bikers, gang-bangers, or giggling college girls looking at stacks of binders. It also lacked the big neon signs announcing what the proprietors did for a living. Instead, it looked more like one of those skin-repair/beauty shops popping up all over the place, with the designer interior and a fresh-faced girl working the counter. In plain speak, the tattoo shop blended into its environment. A chameleon.

Walking through the doors, Luce recognized the faint hum of a tattoo gun camouflaged under the bass of the tech music. A petite, attractive Asian girl wearing a long-sleeve lab coat sat behind the desk, barely looking at Luce to greet her

"Good morning. How may I help you?"

Luce glanced around the pale room. White carpet met white couches and drapes, creating a homogeneous environment, punctuated by a few Lucite tables. It had more of a spa feel than that of a tattoo parlor. A petite woman with bleached-out hair, who obviously had too much money and not enough *things*, sat on a pale-white couch clutching an oversized purse, dressed in a sleeveless frock with its sheer peek-a-boo opening and designer heels, thumbing through the latest celebrity rag. Her porcelain skin was the perfect canvas for the right artist.

Tattoos were the up-and-coming body accessory for everyone, including the rich and famous, and the rich—like everything else they did—built studios that looked more like shrines, lacking the requisite skull art, mirrors, black walls, and fast-paced lives of traditional tattoo shops. Their artists were the Rembrandts and Renoirs of the tattoo world, lured by big money and contact with the moneyed one percent. A lucrative gig like this guaranteed their names would be spoken within those tight circles that hosted cocktail parties, ensuring their names would be passed like cocaine.

"Excuse me. How can I help you?"

Luce dropped her gaze from the porcelain china doll in the corner and focused on the Lancôme lady.

"I'm hear to see Horiyama."

"I'm sorry. I don't know that name."

Luce stiffened, and in her no-nonsense voice she said lowly, "He's expecting me."

"If you'll wait right here, I'll get my boss."

"You do that."

Luce leaned against the counter and checked the shop out, again. Cameras surveilled the entire room, a precaution she was sure was repeated throughout the shop. She glanced at the one strategically placed behind the counter and smiled. She'd been seen the moment she entered and probably the minute she entered the parking lot. It paid to know who was coming and going in these high-dollar suites. A Mercedes received more attention than what was required of someone driving a Jeep onto the property. Both had people interested in their comings and goings, but just one had security attached to it.

Luce pulled her phone and tapped out a quick text to Brooke.

Ready to be sprung from that place? See you in an hour, baby!"

"How may I help…" A well-dressed man in a button-down shirt, black vest, and slacks with his sleeves rolled up and wearing black latex gloves spoke. "Oyabun," he said, bowing deeply. "Welcome. How may I be of service?"

"Hello, Horiyama. I've come to ask you some questions about a tattoo."

"Oh, are you looking to get one?" It was clear he was anticipating the possibility of inking the Yakuza boss.

"No. I already have ink, but I was hoping you could tell me who might have designed a particular one, and perhaps you can tell me its meaning."

"Well, I am almost done with a client. If you'd like to sit in my office, I can have tea brought, and we can look at it together. Do you mind waiting?"

"Not at all. Thank you, Miss…" Luce tossed a terse look at the girl and walked past her.

"Yeow." She bowed slightly.

"I have a woman in my employ with that name. Perhaps you are related?"

"I doubt it," she said dismissively.

"You're right. She has much better manners."

"My apologies, Oyabun. My niece has no idea of our culture. I will correct her behavior and educate her on your position."

"Not to worry. This generation is mindless of our culture and rituals." Luce worried what the master artist would do to his niece, so she downplayed the incident.

Luce was guided past a client reclining in a disjointed position. Her labored breathing as the tattoo artist applied the hissing machine to her skin made Luce wonder if the woman was giving birth or getting ink. She groaned and then started to huff again. Tears were streaming down her determined face, but it was clear she wouldn't last much longer.

The cubicle was nothing like the studio in Japan where Luce got her tat. It had taken several trips for the intricate dragon she carried on her body to be finished to her liking. The studio was etched in her mind, a rite of passage of a young Yakuza who had no idea about her place in the Yakuza world. If her grandfather had had his way, she would never have entered that world, but now she was in, fully.

"I hope this is acceptable, Oyabun?" the man said, ushering her into a simply decorated room. "I'll have tea brought in immediately."

"Thank you."

A few moments later the young woman knocked on the office door.

"Come in."

"My apologies, Oyabun. I have brought tea. I hope it is to your liking."

"I'm sure it will be fine," Luce said. Looking up, she was surprised to see a visible handprint on the young woman's cheek. "Who did that?"

"My apologies for my disrespect earlier. I had no idea who you were." She poured the tea without looking at Luce. "My disrespect has earned me...this," she said, touching her cheek gently.

"I'm sorry. No one deserves to be struck." Luce took the offered cup. "Thank you."

"Thank you," she said, bowing and retreating

quickly.

Luce cradled the small teacup in her hands as she walked around the small office. Japanese paintings graced two of the walls, and delicate statuary flanked a vase. Opposite, a bonsai tree stood simply on an ornamental stand. The size of the trunk told Luce it was old. It needed no wire wrap to train it to bend to the will of the owner anymore. The willow was as graceful in miniature as it would have been full-sized. A small pruning set lay out, meticulously in order, on a swatch of embroidered cloth. As Luce looked around the office, she noted everything had a use in the small, efficient space. Nothing extra filled the shelves or adorned the desk. It was functional and well ordered, just as she assumed the master tattoo artist would be.

"Oyabun, I'm free now. What can I assist you with?"

Now the man seemed nervous as he bowed and offered his hand. She had to wonder at the change. Had he called someone? Should she be on alert?

"I have some pictures I'd like you to look at and tell me what they mean and who the artist is." If she could find out just a few details, she could search out the tattoo artist and question him.

"Of course. I'd be happy to help."

She handed him the jump drive she'd transferred the pictures on, and his hands shook as he grabbed it.

"I took these with my phone, so I hope the quality is good enough."

"I'm sure it will be, Oyabun."

Horiyama pulled his glasses down to the tip of his nose and stared at the computer screen, clicking on the first file in the set.

"Oh, hmm," he muttered as he enlarged the

screen. "Interesting. These are *wabori* style."

"Traditional. Do you know the artist?"

He didn't respond, only enlarging the picture further and then pushing his face closer to the screen. He clicked on the next image and then the next before he said anything.

"This tattoo is incomplete."

"What?" Luce moved closer to the screen and followed his delicate finger as he traced the lines of the tattoo. "This phrase is missing something. Perhaps it isn't finished?"

"I'm not following."

"If I'm translating the kanji correctly, it says, *Blood is binding for a family, even in death.* As you can see, some words are missing."

"Hmm." It was Luce's turn to be perplexed. "What about the symbolism in the tattoo?"

"Ah, yes. The artwork is masterfully done. Look at the cherry blossoms the dragon holds in one claw. Cherry blossoms symbolize rebirth or life. Within the scroll work...look here..." He pointed to a Kanji symbol Luce hadn't seen within the dragon's scales. "*Kakushibori.* The tattoo has some hidden words. This means revenge, and here..." He moved his finger up the screen and traced out another hidden symbol. "This is the symbol for death." He sucked in a breath, pushed his glasses back up his nose, and leaned away from the monitor as if it would bite him. "Someone is sending a powerful curse. It is to you, Oyabun?" He leaned away from her as he gazed up.

"It would seem so."

"Oyabun, someone isn't just sending a message. They are putting a curse on you and your family. To do it on the skin of another is—"

Luce held up her hand to stop his ranting. Clearly, he was upset by what he'd seen.

"If you believe in that sort of stuff," Luce said, her voice laced with sarcasm.

She didn't put that much stock in the old ways of sending curses or binding souls to objects, especially tattoos. Now Auntie, she was a different story. It was probably a good thing she hadn't shown her the tattoo yet. Auntie was the authority on the Korean side of curses and spooks.

"Thank you, Horiyama. I appreciate your help, and I hope I can count on your discretion in this matter?" Luce bowed and grabbed her jump drive from his computer.

"Of course, Oyabun." He stood so quickly he almost dumped his chair backward. Bowing, he said, "Please. I feel that, while you don't follow the old ways, I would be remiss if I didn't tell you that someone is sending you a bad omen. An assassin is looking for you. It says so within the tattoo."

"I understand." She bowed and started to leave.

He grabbed her sleeve. When she looked down at his hand, he withdrew it and apologized. "My apologies, Oyabun, but this is serious."

"Thank you, Horiyama. I appreciate the warning. I'm in your debt." Luce stopped as she reached the door. "May I give you some advice?"

"Of course, Oyabun."

Luce narrowed her gaze, and in a low, ominous tone, she imparted a few words of warning. "Never strike a woman again. I shall be back to check on your niece, and if she is harmed or missing, you and I," she pointed back and forth between them, "will have a short conversation. Do you understand my meaning?"

"Of course, Oyabun. My apologies for my actions."

"A dog that is beaten eventually turns on the hand that feeds it, regardless of how much food you provide. So make sure you treat her as you would treat me. Understand? My second will be by later this week to check on her."

"Yes, Oyabun."

"If I have any other questions, I'll be back."

"Of course, Oyabun." He bowed again, dropping his gaze to the floor. While he wasn't part of her family, it was courteous to abide by the word of an oyabun. He would do as she asked or pay the price for the disrespect.

Luce walked out the way she came, passing the same woman in almost the same position, still huffing out her pain.

"Jesus," Luce said when she finally looked at the grotesque tattoo. She would have to have that shit on her body for the rest of her life. "Too much money and not enough style," Luce said, loud enough for both the artist and the woman to stare at her in disbelief.

Reaching the front desk, Luce stopped and leaned against the hefty piece of furniture.

"Oyabun," Ms. Yeow said.

"Ms. Yeow, I've spoken with your uncle. If he touches you again…" Luce pulled one of her business cards from her jacket and handed it to her. "Call me."

Turning it over and over, the young woman gave Luce a puzzled look.

"Hold it up to the light."

"Aw, clever, Oyabun."

"An oyabun must have some privacy."

"Of course," she said, bowing. "Thank you."

Luce didn't say anything further. Her mind was suddenly clouded with what the old man had confessed. Someone was out to kill her and had sent a very personal calling card.

Chapter Seven

Luce jerked her SUV into the parking garage at the hospital and noticed another car swing in behind her. That alone wasn't surprising, but this sedan had been following her since she left her office. Slipping past the first available spot, she expected the car to grab it if the driver was really there for a reason.

It didn't.

She could gun it, but the SUV sat low for a reason. The armor plating made it a rolling tank, not a Ferrari. She didn't panic, yet. Slowing down to a crawl, she cut the turn tight so she could see the car on the other side of the lane. Blacked-out windows eliminated the opportunity to ID her creeper.

One good thing—that eliminated the feds. Besides, if Colby Water wanted something, she had Luce's number. She could just call.

Calmly, Luce pulled her Nano and placed it on the console between the two seats. Her hand never left the gun. Why had she taken a car without a driver?

Damn.

At least there would've been two of them. Her mind had been off lately. She'd been focused on Brooke, and she kept thinking about the possibility of JP still being alive and having a little sister, who'd just happened to show up with a creepy tattooed message. Okay, so she wasn't exactly on top of her game. Gripping her gun, she reached up and fingered the nav system.

"Dial Sammy."

The automated navigation voice came on and repeated, "Dialing Sammy."

"Hello, Yukon phone," Sammy joked.

"Not funny."

"Sorry, Boss," he said apologetically.

"Sammy, I have a dark sedan on my ass. California plates B6DE88 —"

"Where are you, Oyabun? I'm on my way." She heard him snap his fingers, and chairs skidding across a cement floor echoed through the phone.

"I'm in the hospital parking garage. You're not going to get here in time."

"Well, at least you have Leo with you."

"I drove myself."

"Shit. We're on our way."

Before Luce could say anything else, she turned the corner to drive up another tier. In the middle of the garage, another car was parked, blocking her path forward. Two men, in dark suits, stood on each end of the car. Their hands were crossed in front of them, and sunglasses covered their eyes. The sun had dipped down long ago, so they looked stupid in their gangster-wannabes style. Glancing in her rearview mirror, she watched the car behind her stop, so close she couldn't see the plate. Tapping the nav screen, she turned on her rear camera. The plate filled the screen. Pulling her phone she snapped a picture and sent it to Sammy.

"Boss?"

"I'm blocked in, Sammy."

"Shit."

Luce gripped the Nano tighter in her leather-clad hand and slid her finger onto the trigger. Looking down at the illegal extra-long clip, she knew it would give her enough shots to make it a challenge to whoever was sitting in the car in front and behind her. The extra armor in the car would protect her if she just wanted to wait it out. In her line of work, it was better to be prudent than cocky.

"Boss, Boss," Sammy said, sounding frantic.

"Get security to Brooke's room and send whoever's guarding her to the seventh floor in the garage."

"You got it."

"End call," she said, eyeing her front and rear.

No one moved.

Desperate for a solution, she weighed all possible options. She could gun it and ram the car, clearing a path, or reverse it and crush what was behind her and take her chances. Neither option was prudent. Besides, this might be the time to practice patience and wait for the opposition to make the first move.

Tapping the nav again, she activated the forward and rear cameras on the SUV and hit record. Whoever this was, he was leaving a nice, tidy record for Luce's men to find if anything happened to her. She had Sammy to thank for the technology additions to her office, home, and vehicles. She'd had them installed after the attack on Brooke because she wasn't willing to risk anyone's life ever again.

Luce didn't care what happened next. She'd wait them all out until hell froze over with a thick sheet of ice. She was transfixed on the door to the sideways sedan as it opened. Movement caught Luce's eye. Two more men got out of the car on the farthest side and drew their guns. Taking up positions at the hood and the trunk, the men in front of her reached into their jackets and stopped when the rear window of the sedan rolled down a pinch. One of the thugs bent down to say something into the crack and then pulled the door handle. A slender, long leg, ending in a foot shod in a black stiletto, touched the floor. A woman stood, more like a child's doll, looking directly at Luce as she adjusted her short black dress that barely covered her ass. A short fur coat was pulled tight around her as the woman motioned with her finger to Luce. Petrov must have dived deep into his collection of prostitutes, because this one was so young and petite, Luce wondered if she was even old enough to drink.

Luce shook her head and gripped her gun tighter as she motioned the woman toward her. The woman climbed, with help, out of her car. Throwing a cigarette to the ground, she crushed it under the red tip of her Luboutin shoe, then looked at Luce and motioned for Luce to come over.

Luce shook her head, again. "Persistent, bitch, isn't she?" she muttered to herself.

She wasn't about to expose herself and leave the protective cocoon she was in. The woman opened her jacket and spun around to show Luce she didn't have anything on her person. Luce shook her head again, so the woman started walking toward her SUV. The two men started to follow her, but she said something that made them stop and move back to the car.

As the woman walked down the slight incline, her hips swayed seductively with each step she took. Something was familiar about her, the auburn hair cut in way that flattered her oval face. She smiled as she walked over, tapped the passenger window, and looked at Luce. Luce pointed her gun at the woman, flipped the window control, and dropped it enough that they could have a conversation.

"Hello," she said, spotting the gun pointed at her. "Please. You wouldn't shoot an unarmed woman, now would you." It was more of a statement than a question.

"How do I know you're not carrying something between your legs?"

The woman pulled her wrap off, tossed it onto the hood of the SUV, turned slowly, and then bent down.

"Do you see anything?"

"Between your legs," Luce said, keeping a gun on the woman while watching the cameras out of the corner of her eye.

The woman stepped back, put her hands on her thighs, and slipped the tight dress up. Stockings, old-fashioned garters, and red lace panties peeked out from underneath. Luce's reward for being inquisitive. It also proved Luce could be wrong about female accoutrements.

"Happy?"

"What can I do for you?"

"I would like to see my daughter," she said in a thick Russian accent.

Chapter Eight

"Nurse, can I get something to sleep, please?" Brooke said into the call button on her bed.

"Absolutely, Ms. Erickson. I'll bring it right in."

"Thank you."

Brooke needed to sleep. The exchange with Colby had been frustrating on one level, and on another, well, it only reaffirmed Brooke's earlier comment to Luce—she didn't want to be in Luce's business.

"The doctor thought you might want something to sleep, considering you requested less pain meds."

"That's why he's the doctor," Brooke said just as she popped the sleeping pill into her mouth. "It's been a long, draining day. I think I just need to sleep and hope he releases me soon. I should do much better at home."

"I know what you mean. The constant checking of vital signs, charting, and everything else we have to do can be annoying. Be glad you aren't in a double room. It's twice the aggravation."

"Then I won't complain. Thanks again."

"Of course. I'll see if I can delay rounds for a little while so you can sleep."

"Oh, don't break the rules for me. I'm sure once I'm out, I'll be down for the count."

Looking at Brooke's chart, the nurse responded, "Yeah, this is a strong dose, so you should be out in no time."

"Good."

"Just ring me if you need anything."

"Thanks." Brooke turned slightly on her side away from the door and asked, "Would you mind closing the blinds and turning the lights off?"

"No problem." The room went dark and so did Brooke's mind.

Brooke's awareness swam between periods of lucidness and emptiness as a voice called to her.

"Ms. Erickson, can you hear me?"

Fingers snapped over Brooke's head.

"Huh?"

The room had an ethereal feel as she tried to focus on the voice. God, her dreams were so real lately. Lynn calling to her, to help her. Luce standing over her reassuring her she would be all right. Now some man was calling to her. What the heck?

"Ms. Erickson, you do favor for Petrov, yes?"

"Who?" She struggled to wake up.

"Petrov. Surely you remember me? I'm the man at the warehouse." She raised her eyelid, and a face only a few inches from her filled her field of vision.

Petrov. Shit.

How did he get in here, in her dream? He was one of the few people in all of the hell from the last few weeks that she didn't think about. Suddenly, here he was front and center in her dream. At least she thought it was a dream. Brooke struggled to find the call button. She needed help, since he was the reason she was in here in the first place.

Where was the man on guard at the door? She turned to look in that direction, but Petrov held her head.

"There's emergency in parking garage. Don't

worry. He'll be back and I'll be long gone."

"What the hell do you want?" She jerked her head from his grasp.

Sitting down, he scooted the chair closer and whispered, "Tell Potter that I'm coming for her. She can't protect you, as you can see." If he was trying to scare her, he was succeeding. "I'm going to pay her back for fucking with my business. If you see that agent, what her name is, I don't remember, but tell her I'm coming for her, too."

"I'm not your messenger," Brooke squeaked out.

"I thought you might say that, so I'm leaving a note, just in case you forget."

Panicking, Brooke started to yell. "Nurse, nurse. Help, someone help."

Petrov clamped his hand over her mouth. "Shut the fuck up. I'm not going to hurt you, dumb bitch."

Brooke opened her mouth just enough that one of his fingers slipped in. She bit the knuckle as hard as she could and then pushed him off her with what strength she could muster. The call button slipped from his hand as he reached for the bedrail. Grabbing it, she punched it and screamed again.

"Nurse, help. Someone's in my room. Nurse, nurse."

"Ms. Erickson." A voice on the other end sounded just as frantic. "I'm on my way."

"You better get the hell out of here."

A slap was her reward for being so defiant. "You tell Potter, Petrov is waiting."

Then he was gone.

Brooke laid on the call button, and suddenly a flashback to the warehouse where she had been held snapped in her mind.

Help!

"I'm sorry. I have no idea what you're talking about," Luce lied. She suspected the well-adorned woman was Kat's mother.

"Don't play possum with me, Miss Potter. I might have trouble with English, but not its intent." She nodded to the men in front, who raised their guns, pointing them directly at Luce.

"Mrs. Petrov —"

"Ah, so you do know who I am."

"Mrs. Petrov, I think the word you might be struggling with is coy—"

"Whatever, you get meaning."

"Trust me. I would never play coy with someone such as you," Luce said. "You didn't need to go to all of this trouble. You could've just called my office —"

"I did. I left message after message, but no response."

"Well, you see I've been busy nursing my wife back to the living after the brutal attack at the hands of your husband."

Mrs. Petrov stood with her mouth agape for a brief instance before composing herself. "I don't believe you," she insisted.

Luce raised her left hand, pointing at the men around them. "Somehow, I find that statement ridiculous, considering the firepower you brought with you. You could just ask me how your daughter's doing."

"I have you at a distinct disadvantage, Miss Potter."

Luce shifted the gun into her left hand and looked at Mrs. Petrov. "Do you now?" Luce smiled, and with lightning-fast reflexes, she reached over and grabbed Mrs. Petrov's wrist and yanked her petite body partway through the now-open window and into the SUV. "I guess your husband got all the brains."

"I'll have you skinned and then fed to my dog, you bitch." Mrs. Petrov battled at Luce's grip on her wrist. "Release me immediately, and I'll consider letting you live."

Luce smiled at the woman's word usage and her haughtiness. There was no other word for what Mrs. Petrov had done. Maybe stupid. Okay, she'd go with stupid, too. Whispering, Luce moved closer, pointing the gun at Mrs. Petrov's head as the suited-up beefcake took a few steps closer.

Luce whispered, "Now, tell them to put their guns down, or I'll decorate the inside of my car with your brains."

Mrs. Petrov struggled to pull herself free. Putting her knee against the door, she jerked but only succeeded in pushing herself farther into Luce's SUV. Luce threaded her fingers into Mrs. Petrov's hair, scratching her skull as she clamped down on the fake red locks. This close, Luce could tell the drapes wouldn't be matching the carpet.

"That was a foolish thing to do. Get in the fucking car." Luce yanked the woman's head around and stared at her. "Get the fuck in," she said through clenched teeth.

Mrs. Petrov dropped her ass into the seat, her legs hanging out of the window for a moment, her shoes dropping to the garage floor with a plop, as Luce started to raise the window. She wouldn't need them where she was going. Luce put the window up and watched the men all around her. This game of chess would have only one winner—Luce Potter.

Luce's phone rang. "What?"

"Boss, Petrov was in Brooke's room."

"What?"

"My man just got to the room, and security is crawling all over the floor looking for him. The nurse said he slapped Brooke."

"That fuckin' bastard." Luce pointed the gun at Mrs. Petrov's head and started her car. "This was all a diversion, wasn't it?"

"I have no idea what you're talking about."

"The fuck you say." Luce revved the SUV and started for the sedan in front of her. "Tell them to move or your brains are going to decorate my interior. NOW." She shoved the gun harder against Mrs. Petrov's temple.

Mrs. Petrov waved her hand frantically, trying to get the men to move.

Luce hit the nav console, the phone ringing Sammy, again.

"Boss?"

I'm going to ram these bastards, and then I want you to come and take Mrs. Petrov to our safe house."

"Boss?"

"Just do as I say. I'm going to get Brooke out of here. She isn't safe. I'll call you when I get her home, and we'll change out the men guarding Mrs. Petrov."

"Yes, Oyabun."

"Sammy?"

"Boss?"

"Never mind." She wasn't going to say much with Petrov's wife sitting right next to her.

"Boss, what about the package at the house?"

"I'll take care of that. You just meet me at the bottom of the garage. Send Momo over with a car so I can take Brooke home."

"You got it,"

Luce could hear Sammy running and barking orders to someone. Then the line went dead. Gunning the car, she headed straight for the sedan. The men scattered as she hit the sedan mid-body.

"Now, tell them to move it and don't follow, or they'll have to tell your husband how I blew your head off." Luce lowered the window a smidge. Mrs. Petrov yelled something in Russian to the men, and the car moved enough for Luce to wedge her way around it and back down the spiral cement raceway. "I'm going to kill that bastard, and you better hope he didn't fuck with my girlfriend, or I'm going to do to you what he did to her," Luce spit out.

Chapter Nine

Luce ran up the stairs, too impatient to wait for the elevator. Adrenaline guided her feet, and she grabbed the rail for assistance until she hit the fourth floor. Down the hall, she spotted four men and Momo standing outside Brooke's door.

"Where is she?" Luce didn't wait for an answer as she threaded her way past the hulk. "Brooke?"

"Here?" Brooke's frail voice drifted from beyond the people surrounding the bed. "Luce?"

"Honey, I'm right here," Luce said, pushing someone out of the way. "Baby, are you—"

The red handprint on Brooke's face blazed like a neon sign. Petrov had hit her hard enough that the blow would leave a bruise. Luce's stomach lurched. She had promised Brooke, she would protect her, yet Petrov had found a way in to her hospital room. Obviously, he'd been watching her every move and used his wife as a diversion. He wanted her to know he could get to her and wasn't above using his wife or Brooke to send a message. Well, his little plan had backfired. He hadn't anticipated Luce grabbing his wife. Now it was her turn to rotate the table and put him on the receiving end of some punishment.

She'd have to stow that idea. She needed to think about Brooke and getting her the fuck out of here.

"How did this happen," she asked no one in particular. The crowd widened, away from Luce. A doctor focused on Brooke, checking her pupils and then rotating her face so he could look at the bruise that was now starting to purple.

"I want some fucking answers," Luce said in a low growl.

"Baby, calm down. It isn't anyone's fault." Brooke grabbed for Luce's hand and held it tight. Brooke was the lifeline in Luce's tilting ship, the one thing that kept her anchored to the normal world. Otherwise, Luce was certain she would sink into the darkness of the gangster life. In the beginning, her grandfather had been that person, but as he lay in his hospital bed, he had given Luce the sagest of advice.

"Kaida, let me give you a few last words of wisdom from an old man." Tamiko licked his dry, cracked lips and swallowed hard. He labored to breathe as he continued to speak. *"Kaida, as a tree struggles to find purchase in a granite rock, it grows without assistance. It finds life where none should exist in the cracks of the hard rock, determined to grow, even when it should be impossible. Brooke is the tree to your rock. She gives you shade, grows with you when others would perish, and finds nourishment in your soul."*

"She's a wonderful woman, Grandfather."

"Then marry her. You are in a place now that will cause those around you to test you. You will find out when I die who is an ally and who is an enemy. Just as Frank betrayed us, others will, too. They will tell lies and make you doubt the truth when you are faced with it." Gently, he patted her hand in reassurance. *"Brooke is your strongest supporter. Don't let her go, Kaida. She's wonderful for you. Good for your soul. I can see she softens your rough edges."*

He was right. Brooke was the tree in the rock of her existence.

"Honey, I'll be fine," Brooke reassured Luce.

"I know you will, sweetheart. Because I'm taking you out of here."

"Doctor, I'd like you to write some discharge orders. Orders for scripts and anything else she might need. Then I'd like you to come and check on her in the morning and evening."

"But—"

"Otherwise, I'm going to sue the shit out of this hospital, and you don't have deep-enough pockets. Look at her. Tell me you can protect her. She's obtained another injury while under the care of this hospital." Luce paused, took a deep breath, and gentled her voice. "If you can't see to her, then recommend a concierge doctor. Someone that can be trusted."

"Of course. I'll personally attend to her care, Ms. Potter. I'm so sorry."

Luce knew he was throwing himself on his sword. Anything to protect the hospital from a lawsuit.

"Fine. Now let's get you ready to go home, honey." Luce sat on the bed and cupped Brooke's face. She wanted to cry, but no way would she let her guard down in front of everyone. Instead, she bit the inside of her mouth, the taste of blood more appropriate for the moment.

※ ※ ※ ※

Brooke tried her best to reassure Luce, but right now wasn't the time to say anything other than yes. Actually, going home sounded like a wonderful idea.

She was feeling claustrophobic with everyone leaning over her.

"I'm looking forward to being at home. I want to sleep in my own bed and just rest."

"Agreed. Home it is, sweetheart."

"Um, Boss, what about the package at the house?" Momo pushed a few people back to make way for his girth.

"I'll take care of it." Luce never took her eyes off Brooke.

"What's going on at home, Luce?" Brooke whispered.

Brooke didn't like surprises, and if Luce had something in mind, she wanted to put a kibosh on it right now. All she wanted was to lie in her own bed with her lover beside her. No surprises, no overly excessive, fawning nurses, and no one else paid to worry about her.

"Would everyone mind and give us some privacy? Please." Luce commanded the room, and the room emptied. Brooke wondered that if Luce stood next to water, would it too part?

Finally, the room was silent and still. Brooke leaned back against the bed and scrutinized her partner. Something was up, but pushing Luce would put in place a certain law of physics—anything pushed will push back with equal force, except for Luce, who pushed harder.

"Luce?"

Luce grabbed Brooke's hand and lifted it to her lips. Uh-oh. This wasn't going to be good. Tenderness before bad news always equaled trouble.

"I just found out I might have a sister," Luce blurted out.

"What? How?"

A side glance from Luce and a half smile accompanied her response. "I have no idea."

"How did you find out?"

"That little issue I had to take care of? Well, it turns out she showed up at the office with a message."

"A message?" Brooke felt like she was searching in the darkness for answers to questions that were more like riddles.

"She has a tattoo on her back, more like a message, for me. It's signed by JP."

"JP! How is that possible?"

Luce shrugged.

"Where is she?"

"At the house."

"Your house?"

"Our house."

"Maybe it would be better if I went to my place. It might be a little crowded, and you look like you need to get to the bottom of this, honey." Brooke patted Luce's hands.

"I'm not letting you go anywhere without me. Understand?"

"But…perhaps you need to find out about this sister thing, and I'll only be in the way."

"I'm not making that mistake again. Besides, I like it when you're in the way. That's the only time I know where you are now." Luce kissed her hand again and avoided making eye contact.

"Look at me, Luce." Brooke slipped her finger under Luce's chin and lifted Luce's face so they were eye-to-eye. "You're not responsible for what happened to me and Lynn. That's Frank's fault, so let's end that guilt trip right now before you start packing more bags for extended travel."

"I'm not taking you to your house. End of discussion."

"That's fine. I just don't want to be a burden. Now with this sister thing, I don't want you to feel like you have to worry about me."

"Good, then you'll stay at our house and I won't have to worry. I'll be able to take care of you and make sure you're safe while I clear up another little..." Luce squeezed her finger and thumb together. "Problem I have."

"What problem would that be?"

"Well, I just kidnapped Petrov's wife. Best I can figure out, the bitch had me blocked in while her husband was up here threatening you."

"What? You've got to be kidding me."

"On which part?" Luce shot Brooke a side-eye glance.

"Oh, God, Luce. What do you think he's going to do now that you have both his wife and his daughter?"

"If he's smart, nothing."

"Luce."

"I'm sorry, honey. Who knew it would be so fortuitous that I ran into her in the garage. I reacted, and now I'm glad I did. He's going to pay for threatening you. He's out of control, and I intend to end his little reign of terror."

Brooke had an uneasy feeling about all this. Luce was right. Petrov was out of control, but she was afraid Luce had just provoked a hibernating bear even more than an early spring would. This wasn't going to end well. She was sure of that.

"Oh, I just remembered. He asked me to give you a message," Brooke said, slipping Luce a folded piece of paper.

After opening it, Luce's eyes narrowed, and her jaw bunched as her eyes followed each word. She wadded up the piece of paper and squeezed her fist.

Brooke touched Luce's face. "What did it say?"

"He's a dead man." That was all Luce would offer. "Come on. Let's get you home."

Chapter Ten

Luce gently lifted Brooke into the backseat of the SUV and then walked to the other side to sit next to her, still clenching Petrov's note in her fist.

The doctor's orders were easy to follow—no baths, rest, get up every two hours, stretch, and walk. Blood clots were an issue, given her lack of mobility. Taking painkillers had kept Brooke bedridden for most of her stay in the hospital, but now that she was going home, she needed to be up and moving.

Lacing her fingers with Brooke's, she held her hand and pretended to study the scenery as it passed by. It held little interest for Luce as she thought about the note and how she was going to handle Petrov's wife. Sammy had taken her and Kat to Luce's cabin in Marin, which no one knew about. It was Luce's hideaway when she needed to duck out of town and avoid all that technology offered in her day-to-day life. Electricity, a shortwave radio from the previous owner, and a TV attached to an antenna were it for modern technological conveniences. Now that she knew they were tucked away safely, she could use them to bargain for Frank. That is, if Petrov valued their lives. If he didn't, if they were replaceable, then Luce would have a problem. But for now, she had only one worry—to get Brooke home and tucked safely in bed.

"You know what sounds good?" Brooke asked.

"No, my love. What sounds good?" She expected

Brooke to say something like ice cream or a burger from Dave's Joint.

"A swim?"

"What?" Not what Luce was expecting at all. "Doctor's orders—no baths, yet."

"I know, but I'm healing well." Brooke pulled the bandage back and looked at the stitches.

Luce looked away, her stomach rolling. She couldn't handle looking at wounds, stitches, or anything that oozed.

"I'm sorry. I know how you get when—"

"I'm fine." Blood, yes. Open stab wounds, no problem. But this, yuk."

"It's covered, sweetheart."

"Thanks." Luce pulled her hankie from her inside jacket pocket and wiped the cold sweat from her brow. She caught Momo looking at her in the rearview mirror. "Can I help you, Momo?"

"Sorry, Boss. I just wanted to let you know that we've had a sedan on our ass since we left the hospital."

Luce turned around to see for herself, but the tint on the windows did just as much to keep light out as it did to block her line of sight.

"Luce?"

"It'll be all right." Luce squeezed Brooke's hand for assurance and then looked back at Momo. "Call Sasha."

"You got it." Momo hit the nav system, and Sasha popped on the line.

"Oyabun?"

"Sasha, where are you?"

"I'm with Sammy. I just dropped Kat off with him, and we're loading up the car right now."

"Get Leo to go with Sammy. I need backup. We're

on…Momo?"

"West, coming up on Lincoln."

"Did you hear that?"

"Yes, ma'am."

"Meet us at West and Washington. Momo, we're going to take our tail for a little drive, then head to Washington. How long will it before you can get there?"

"Ten minutes tops, Boss."

"Sasha, good. I want you to wedge in between us and the sedan and do whatever it takes to slow them down. Then break off and meet us at the house."

"You got it."

"And Sasha, be careful." Luce didn't want to lose another of her family.

"Yes, Boss."

"Momo, I feel like a drive through Medford Heights."

"Yes, Oyabun."

"Luce?" Brooke's hand trembled in hers.

"It'll be okay. I promise."

Luce let Brooke's hand go. She pulled her gun and set it on the seat between them. Reaching for Brooke's hand again, she worried that in Brooke's state, she might freak out, so she pulled her closer.

"Once Sasha gets here, we'll take you home and tuck you in bed. I just don't want any strays hanging around." She laughed and then gently threaded her fingers in Brooke's hair and kissed her head. "I'm not going to let anyone touch you, sweetheart. Momo, call Agent Water, please."

"Yes, ma'am."

"Is that necessary?"

"I think so."

The phone rang through and Colby answered. "This better be important, Potter."

"Sweet. You have me in your phone-a-friend data base. I'm touched."

"Potter—"

Luce changed her tone immediately. "Agent Water, there was a situation at the hospital today with Brooke." She didn't want Colby to think this was some sort of social call.

"Is she all right?"

"She's fine, now."

Brooke piped up. "I'm all right."

"What the hell happened?"

"Petrov showed up and threatened her life."

"Fuck me."

"While that's an inviting offer, I'm afraid I'm going to have to turn it down, Agent Water."

"Funny, Potter. Where are you now?"

"Heading home, but I have a bit of a problem."

"Don't tell me you have a friend?"

"Exactly."

"Where are you?"

"Not to worry. I have someone on the way to run interference so I can get Brooke home, but I might need you to help my associate once she gets them off us."

"Where is she picking up the tail?"

"West and Washington."

"Got a plate number for me by any chance?"

"Momo?"

"Sorry, Boss."

"That's a no, but perhaps you can call someone to help Sasha out. Perhaps the local PD can do a stop-and-frisk."

"Am I going to find anything if I send out the big dogs?"

"Probably illegal guns, at a minimum."

"Got a description for me at least?"

"Momo?"

"Black Saab, four-door limousine, tinted windows, and two guys in the front seat. Caucasian."

"We'll be at West and Washington in about ten minutes. Sasha will be in a dark SUV. Let's make sure she doesn't get swept up in the stop."

"I'll see what I can do."

"Thank you, Agent Water."

"Anything else, Potter?"

"You don't happen to do delivery, do you?" Luce laughed.

"Nice try. Take care of Brooke."

The line went dead before she could say *of course*.

"Did you have to call Colby?"

Brooke sounded pissed, but Luce wasn't about to lose another member of her family to Petrov.

"I did. I'm sorry, but I need to protect you, and I'll call whatever favor I have, with anyone I know, to make sure you're safe."

"I know. I just wish it wasn't a favor from Colby," Brooke said, resting her head on Luce's shoulder.

"It'll be okay."

The drive through Medford Heights was quick. The luxurious homes were palatial, manicured, and reeking of old money—just the way the one-percenters liked them. Luce didn't envy them. In fact, she pitied their shortsightedness and pompous asses. They worked so hard to keep their money within their upper crust that they all buttered the same bread to keep people like Luce out of their layer. Her money wasn't welcome on that circuit, unless, of course, it was donated to one of the charities or galas they always seemed to be having. Parting people from their money was the kind of tag-team sport they were raised to play. Besides, hosting charity events was almost like working with the poor and underserved. Right?

"There's Sasha, Boss."

"Good. Gun it and then turn left on Van Buren."

"You got it." Luce could see Momo's eyes flash with excitement. He had worked with Luce the least, but the reports she'd received on his job performance were exemplary.

Luce watched as Sasha wedged herself between Luce's SUV and the Saab. As if on cue, red and blues flashed behind the car following Sasha, and then they were out of sight.

"See, easy," Luce whispered into Brooke's hair.

"Hmm. Can we go home now?"

"One more stop, Momo. Dave's Joint. I'm buying."

"You got it, Boss," Momo said a little too enthusiastically.

Chapter Eleven

A burger had never tasted so good, Brooke thought, shoving the last bite into her mouth. Hospital food had its benefits—nutritious, cooked by someone else, and boring. A Dave's Joint burger, on the other hand, was pure heaven, full of bad stuff, and even worse were the sweet potato fries. Fat, soothing goodness. She closed her eyes and enjoyed chewing the last morsel of her burger.

"Good, huh?" Luce said, smiling.

"Hmm, it's beyond good. It's almost orgasmic."

"I wouldn't go that far." Luce rolled her eyes. "I can think of a few other things more orgasmic than a burger, my love."

Brooke poked Luce in the ribs. A girly squeal was her reward as they both laughed at the sound. "Where did that come from?" Brooke asked.

"No idea." Luce sobered when she caught a glance of Momo looking at her in wonder. "This doesn't leave the car, Momo. Understand?"

"Yes, Boss." He went back to attacking his triple-patty heart attack.

"What about your sister? Shouldn't we pick up something for her?"

Luce gave Brooke a puzzled look.

"You are her host, right? You should at least make sure your houseguest is being taken care of. I mean...she is staying at the house, right?"

"Yes, she is, but I'm not sure if she eats American food."

"What? Everyone eats a burger and fries." Brooke could feel Luce's dubious stare. "Well, everyone should eat a burger and fries at least once in their lives."

"Hmm."

"Momo, back through the drive-through."

"Yes, Boss."

"What's she like?"

"Who?" Luce said, sipping from her soda.

"Your sister. What's her name?"

"Mei."

"And?"

"And what?" Luce was being suspiciously vague and avoiding her questions.

"Luce Potter. Stop this right now. What is she like?"

Luce turned and faced Brooke, a stern look her reward for being pushy. "She's young, too young, slim, beautiful, and has a tattoo that's more like a curse."

"A curse?"

"I had someone read it for me earlier, and he says there are hidden kanji symbols within the tattoo, and someone is trying to put a curse on me and my family."

"Do you believe in that stuff?"

"Not really, but Auntie does. I'm going to have her look at it later and give me her take."

"Huh." Brooke let her mind wrap around the idea of someone putting a curse on Luce, and then she wondered what kind of person let someone else tattoo something like that on their skin. The permanence of it all was bewildering to Brooke, who didn't sport a single one.

"Why would anyone let someone else tattoo their

body like that?"

"My question exactly."

"And what did she say?"

"That she was just the messenger. If she didn't deliver the message, she was supposed to kill herself."

"What? That's just outrageous."

"Now you know why I'm so suspicious of her."

"Do you think she's your sister?"

As they pulled through the huge iron gates to Luce's estate, she responded, "I'll let you be the judge of that. We're here."

Suddenly, Brooke was a little afraid to get out of the car and meet this stranger who'd invaded their home. She was sure Luce had been ever the gracious host and offered the residence to Mei, but still it was a little disconcerting.

❊❊❊❊

Luce pulled Brooke into her arms and carried her toward the mansion.

"Luce, honey, I'm perfectly able to walk on my own."

"Nonsense. I'll carry you into the house. Besides…" She pumped Brooke up and down a few times. "It feels like you've lost weight, my love."

"Well, after that burger, it feels like I've gained five pounds, easily."

"Hmm," Luce grunted.

Momo opened the door just as Luce's housekeeper palmed the handle. "Oh, sorry about that," he said, stepping back.

"Ms. Potter, Ms. Erickson, you're finally home," she said, bowing.

"Thank you, Celeste. It's good to be here."

"Celeste, where is our guest?"

"In the guest room, Ms. Potter." Celeste closed the massive door and took Brooke's bag from Momo. "I'm afraid she's only gone between the guest room and the library."

"Has she eaten?"

"She requested tea and some traditional Japanese cuisine. I sent Sammy out for it while he was here."

"Thank you, Celeste."

"Of course, Ms. Potter. How may I be of assistance?"

"I'm good, Celeste," Brooke said before Luce could respond.

"We'll be fine, Celeste."

"Could you put this in the frig, Celeste?" Luce handed her the burger and fries they'd brought Mei.

After Celeste set the bag inside the bedroom door and left, Luce gently set Brooke on the bed and then fell onto it next to her.

"That's the most you've worked out in a while, isn't it?" Brooke giggled.

"Very funny, my waif of a wife."

"You should go check on our guest, Luce."

"I will, but I want to get you settled first."

Brooke looked around the room. "I like what you've done with the place."

"Very funny."

Luce realized she'd seen very little of her home since the attack. It was her sanctuary, her refuge from the outside world, a place she didn't let anyone else in except Brooke.

The window shades were drawn. The darkness of the room beckoned, wrapping Luce in its protective womb even still. The whiteness of the walls and the masculine, heavy furniture were all signatures of Luce's ideal world. Luce prided herself on being in control, strong, and ethnic, qualities reflected in the artwork and statuary as well. Her Japanese/Korean heritage was on display for only her to see. What lived outside these walls was her business life, but what lived inside was her personal life with Brooke.

"Shall I get the bed ready?" Luce asked.

Brooke flashed Luce a puzzled look. "Why are you avoiding introducing me to your sister?"

"I'm not. I'm just trying to make you comfortable."

"Then let's go, and you can introduce me to Mei."

"Are you sure you're up for that?"

"Luce, it isn't like we're going to walk miles. She's just down the hall. Please?" Brooke sounded incensed.

"Fine. Let me change clothes."

"Fine."

Luce flipped the walk-in closet light on and fingered through her wardrobe. What did a person wear when introducing the love of her life to a complete stranger?

A thought pierced Luce's mind. What would Mei think of Luce being with a woman?

Chapter Twelve

Brooke watched her lover pull clothes from their hangers and then put them back. Why was Luce so nervous? Then she wondered how she would act if she found out she had a long-lost sister. One with tattoos that supposedly put a curse on your family?

"Honey, are you all right?" Brooke eased herself off the bed and made her way, slowly, into the closet. "What are you doing?"

Luce sat on the settee with piles of clothes around her. She huffed and then stood in just her underwear. "I have no idea."

Brooke reached into the pile and extracted a sweater and jeans. "Here. These will look fine."

"Thanks." Luce shrugged the sweater on and then slipped into the jeans, buttoned the front, and sat back down.

"What's wrong?"

"I just have a lot on my mind, and I really don't need this right now."

"Need what?"

"A phantom sister. A father back from the undead. A family curse, Petrov, Frank, any of it."

"Then worry about only what you can." Brooke sat next to Luce and wrapped her arm around her shoulder. "I still love you."

Luce offered her a slim smile. "I love you, more

than you'll ever know."

"Wait...a father back from the undead? Are you saying JP might not be dead? How is that possible?"

Luce shrugged. She didn't have a clue and didn't think she had enough vowels to buy one, let alone take an educated guess. "It was something Mei said back at the office, or maybe didn't say. She said we had the same father, and the tattoos are a new thing. A messenger sent her to me. To what? Warn me? Kill me?"

"Don't go letting your mind run away with itself. Try to remain calm, and maybe she can give you some answers."

"Hmm, I doubt it. I think I'm supposed to figure out what the tats mean. Remember, she's just the delivery agent."

"Come on. Let's go meet your sister and see if we can pry something out of her."

Brooke pulled Luce up and guided her down the hall to the library. Somehow she knew that's where Mei would be. At least that's where she should be. Not shut in a bedroom, in a house that wasn't hers. Pushing through the door, they found the library empty.

"Well, I thought she'd be in here," Brooke said.

"Gardens," Luce said.

"Why?"

"That's where I'd be, in the gardens. Meditating or something. At least I know I wouldn't be stuck inside."

Dusk was just setting as they entered the gardens, which were where Luce had spent an enormous amount of time. Each plant had its own marker designating its species and genus. The manicured lawn was like a barrier of lush green roping in all of the beauty. A woman sat on the bench next to the koi pond. She was slight, whereas Luce was mature. Her hair was blond and spiky, whereas Luce's was dark and long, As sisters they were polar opposites of the same coin, at least from this vantage point, Brooke thought. The woman's head was lowered as she studied the fish. Their footsteps on the pea gravel announced their approach.

"*Oneesan,*" Mei said, bowing.

"*Imoutosan,*" Luce said, also bowing. Luce extended her hand toward Brooke and pulled her closer. "This is my girlfriend, Brooke Erickson."

Brooke looked at Luce quizzically.

"Sister," Luce said, answering the unasked question.

"Ms. Erickson." Mei bowed again.

"Mei, may I call you Mei? Or would you prefer Ms. Potter?"

"Mei, please." Mei didn't look at Brooke at first. Her head remained bowed for a short time before she finally did. If she was shocked that Luce was a lesbian, Mei didn't show it. Her reserved demeanor held firmly in place.

Brooke was shocked, though, and sucked in a breath. Mei was definitely Luce's sister. The eyes were identical. The soft jade green was the same, but how could that be? Mei was so much younger than Luce. Finally, Brooke understood why Luce was so skeptical.

"You have beautiful gardens, Oneesan," Mei said so softly that both Luce and Brooke leaned in to hear her.

"Thank you. I enjoy spending time out here, especially during this time of year."

"Yes, spring has the beauty of birth and regeneration. My favorite is autumn, when everything is dying, getting ready to sleep and waiting for a new birth."

Brooke broke into the conversation. "I hope Celeste has made you comfortable in the guest room. Is there anything you need?"

"No, thank you."

"Have you eaten?"

"Yes, thank you."

Luce motioned to the bench, and both of them sat, putting a space between them for Luce.

"Mei, do you mind if I ask you some questions?"

"Of course not, sister."

༄༅༄༅

Luce stood looking down at Brooke and Mei, polar opposites on the spectrum of women. One was her lover, and the other, someone she should have an affinity for, but Luce was having a hard time even admitting Mei was her sister.

"I've had a master tattoo artist familiar with Japanese tattoos and culture look at the photographs of your tattoo."

"I see. Was it to your liking?"

"To my liking?"

"His answers. Did you find the answers to your liking?"

"I'm not sure I would say they were to my liking, but he did explain their meaning, if that's what you're referring to."

"Yes." Mei cast her eyes down to her hands and nervously fidgeted with her fingers.

"Mei, who put the tattoos on your back?" Luce asked.

"Our father had them put on."

"When?"

"A few years ago, when I was younger."

Brooke piped up. "What kind of monster would tattoo a child?"

"I am not as young as you may think, Ms. Erickson."

"Brooke, please."

"As you wish."

"How old were you when he did this to you?"

"Father was convinced this was the only way he could reach you, so he made me the messenger, sister."

"Do you even know what the tattoos mean?"

"I am sure they are a love note from a father to a daughter that he loves."

Mei was either so innocent that she had no clue what their father was like or so brainwashed that it didn't matter what he said. She saw only the positive in their father. Again, assuming she was her sister.

"The tattoos carry a curse within them," Luce said, crossing her arms and looking down at Mei.

"I do not believe that Father would do such a thing. He only spoke lovingly of you, sister," Mei said softly.

"Bullshit," Luce responded.

"Luce." Brooke spoke up. "Perhaps your sister hasn't had the same experience with JP as you have," she said tersely.

Why was Brooke getting mad at her? She'd been the one to deal with her own mother's suicide at the hands of JP. Now she was supposed to believe that she had a secret sister, hidden away all these years. She was calling bullshit on all of this fairy-tale crap. JP was a monster, and nothing good came from a monster like that. Luce should know, for she was his daughter, too.

Everything he touched paid a price for his attention.

"He's dead." Luce stared at her sister, defying her to say different.

"I'm sorry, but he is very much a live, sister."

"I shot him, personally."

"Yes. He wears the bullet holes in his legs with honor," Mei said, looking back defiantly at Luce.

How did she know JP had been shot in the legs? Stunned, Luce wanted to choose her next words wisely. She glanced at Brooke and saw nothing but sympathetic eyes staring back at her. She hadn't told Brooke everything that had happened in the warehouse. Only that JP was dead.

"I'm sure you can prove he's alive."

"My tattoo is a message from our father."

Luce tried a different tactic. "Who's your mother?"

Mei hung her head, tears falling on her clasped hands. "I don't know her."

"How could you not know who your mother is?" Luce asked.

"My father tells me that my mother abandoned us when I was born."

Great, now we're getting into some serious childhood baggage here, Luce thought. Having JP as her father wasn't bad enough. Luce suspected that JP was the one who left, not the mom.

"Have you ever seen your mother or her family?"

"Only once." Mei struggled to speak. "When our father had them sign papers saying they would never come for me. They were disgraced by my mother's behavior and gladly signed the papers giving our father sole custody."

"I see. He was so magnanimous, I suppose. Paid

them handsomely, did he?" Luce felt like punching something, anything to work out the frustration she was feeling at the moment. JP never took care of anything. If Luce were a guessing woman, she'd lay money on the fact that Mei's mom was probably dead somewhere.

"He didn't want them to suffer for what my mother had done to the family."

"Hmm. Why am I not surprised?" Luce turned and walked back to the house. She'd waded through enough bullshit for one day. She needed answers, so it was time to do some investigating. If JP were alive, he'd be making an appearance soon. Did this nightmare never end?

Chapter Thirteen

Brooke was left behind, sitting with Mei. Unsure of what to say, they sat in silence for a few minutes. A sob broke free from Mei, and Brooke scooted over and hugged her.

"Her bark is worse than her bite. Trust me. I know."

"I'm afraid that my sister doesn't believe me about our father. He truly loves her." Mei sniffled.

"I'm sure the man who has raised you is a wonderful person, but Luce's father wasn't around for Luce after her mother died. I'm afraid she had a different experience with JP."

"I see." Mei leaned back, wiped at her nose, and continued speaking. "Perhaps I should go and talk to her?"

"I'd give her some time to think about things." Brooke knew that, in Luce's present state, she was dealing with a lot.

"I see," Mei said again.

"Perhaps you'd like to see some family pictures?"

"Oh, that would be nice. I'm afraid I don't have any."

"That's all right. You can see Luce as a child, and perhaps you'd like to see pictures of your father."

"That would be wonderful." Brooke grabbed Mei's hand, and they walked back to the house. Luce's study contained photos of her grandfather, cousins, aunts and uncles, her mother, and JP. Perhaps knowing where Luce came from would help ease the tension between the two.

"In here. Luce keeps a few mementos and photographs in her study."

"Are you sure it's okay? I would not want Ms. Potter to be upset with me further. I believe I have upset her too much already."

Brooke watched as Mei looked around the room. The small netsuke statues Luce collected caught her attention, and she blushed at the sexually explicit nature of the collection. They had made even Brooke blush when she first saw them. She wasn't surprised at Mei's reaction as she quickly moved past them to study other items Luce owned. Luce had moved the huge embroidered ceremonial kimono from its place at the end of the hall, just outside her study, to its new place of honor in the study. The delicate lighting highlighted the intricate work, and Luce had told Brooke it had been her grandfather's. After his death, she had wanted it for her own enjoyment.

"This is beautiful. I haven't seen work like this since leaving Japan."

"It was Luce's grandfather's. It was a time honored tradition for the men to wear these." Brooke looked again at the kimono "He wore it for ceremonial purposes, from what I understand. It holds a place of honor in Luce's house and was handed down to her when she turned eighteen."

"Her grandfather is no longer living?" Mei said, pressing her face closer to the hermetically sealed box.

"No. Her grandfather died last year." Brooke brought a small photo album over to the couch and patted the seat next to her. "Please, sit."

Mei shuffled over and sat down. Brooke still had a hard time reconciling that the spiky blonde, with jade eyes, could be Luce's sister, but something familiar in the way she handled herself reminded her of Luce.

"These are family photos of Luce as a child. This one," she pointed to a woman and a man together in the black-and-white image, "shows her grandfather and grandmother. He was Oyabun before Luce."

Mei turned her head and stared at the image. "He was Yakuza?"

"Yes."

"Hmm."

Brooke slowly turned the pages as she tried to remember the explanations that went with the photos.

"This is Luce when she was younger." Luce, wearing a school uniform and clutching a small lunchbox, stood beside her mother, who was kneeling. Mother and daughter shared the same broad smile.

The next photo showed a younger JP and Luce's mother. Mei didn't say anything as she studied the shot. She didn't let out a hint of recognition or a squeal of delight, nothing.

"Who is the man?"

Brooke was stunned. She looked at Mei and then back at the photo. Didn't she recognize her own father? Something was off. Turning the page, they came to the next photo, of all the Yakuza clan with a very young Tamiko siting in the middle. His back straight and his hands on his knees, he was wearing the kimono Luce had hanging on the wall, while the men around him were showing off their *irezumi* tattoos. Many of the men in the photo had elaborate chest and arm pieces, while others were barely starting their collection. Tamiko looked stately as he stared into the camera.

"My father," Mei said, pointing to one of the men in the photo.

Brooke recognized him immediately. Frank.

Chapter Fourteen

Sleep evaded Luce. No matter how long she stared at Brooke, she just couldn't shake the feeling something was working against her. Had kidnapping Petrov's wife been a mistake? Not to her. He'd made a big mistake when he sneaked into Brooke's hospital room, and she was relieved fate had delivered his wife to her. Karma was working in her favor, but the universe, well, that was spinning its own tangent around her.

A snap decision.

Luce poured herself two fingers of bourbon and broke out a cigar. Sitting on the couch, she lit up the TV and turned on the surveillance system that ran through her computer. She'd had it upgraded after Brooke's kidnapping, vowing to never be taken by surprise again. The camera ran with an app she could access through her phone so she could check in on the house anytime she was away.

Snipping the end of the cigar, she burnt the end, blew on it, and then took a long puff. She needed her mind to do nothing. No planning, no thoughts of revenge, just be. Blowing out a long trail of smoke, she let her head fall back and followed the tendrils as they reached up and dissipated into the air. She'd shared a cigar or two with her grandfather, brought him a few Cubans back from one of her trips abroad. Illegal, but worth the risk. He'd saved them for their quiet moments together. Now she had the few that were left after his death.

A sip of the whiskey, with its peaty accents, complemented the taste of fine tobacco and burned on its way down. Her new motto was to live life to its fullest. Tomorrow wasn't promised to anyone.

Movement on the screen caught her eye. It was Mei in the pool. She'd offered Mei the complete use of her house. Though her distrust of the woman was ever present, she refused to treat her like a prisoner. It had been Brooke's idea to let her explore, knowing that someone would always be on guard. If anything happened, Luce had to trust her men would be able to handle the situation. Brooke told Luce that eventually she'd have to let someone else handle the heavy lifting of security. So she'd assigned Sasha to watch Mei. Sasha wasn't happy that Luce had taken her off Kat, but Luce was concerned that being Kat's shadow was compromising Sasha's judgment. She'd seen the way Sasha had looked at Kat and recognized the first signs of someone smitten. More movement, and Luce caught sight of Sasha in the background, keeping an eye on Mei.

Relaxing, she took another pull of the cigar and watched Mei swim effortlessly through the water. Mei was definitely an accomplished swimmer. Luce relaxed and took another sip of her bourbon. She'd missed something with Mei, but she couldn't put her finger on it. Mei's mother was Japanese and still alive, but where? Mei wasn't very forthcoming with that information. So Luce would have to do what she did best: put someone on the case.

Colby Water instantly came to mind. Another favor? Possibly, but perhaps she had something she could trade with Colby. She had Petrov's wife, and Petrov, assuming he loved her, might do anything to get her back. Not before Luce exacted a little revenge though. She had plans for Petrov, and he would have to give up Frank before she turned him over to Agent Water.

Luce poured another bourbon and finished her cigar as she skimmed through the camera feeds throughout the house. Then she returned to the swimming pool. Ready to close the feed and head to bed, she noticed Mei was still swimming, but then she stopped and leaned against the pool edge to talk to Sasha. Odd that she would talk to Sasha. She almost seemed relaxed as she tried to chat her up. Unfortunately for Mei, Sasha wasn't the chatty type. Cool and aloof, Sasha simply stood there, her arms crossed, as she just stared at the swimmer. Mei's sudden friendliness seemed out of character, and it bothered Luce. Something was off. What was her angle? Why talk to Sasha? Luce didn't like the sudden change in Mei's personality. From the looks of it, she was almost flirting with Sasha. So much for the cold, disinterested front Mei had been putting up. Luce didn't trust her, and this new wrinkle just added to her suspicions of Mei.

Luce continued to focus on Mei as she began swimming laps again. Then something caught Luce's attention. Zooming the camera in, she watched closer. The lighting in the pool area highlighted something on Mei's back. A hidden design popped in the fluorescent lights of the poolroom. Luce grabbed her phone, hit the app, replayed the security footage, and took a screen shot of the image. She couldn't make it out because of the water drops on Mei's back, but something was definitely there. She mentally tried to dissect the pattern, but it just wasn't clear enough.

She doubted Mei would let her take another look at the tattoo, so she was going to have to come up with another way to get a look at it.

Sasha.

Chapter Fifteen

Brooke tossed and turned, welcoming a few minutes of sleep here and there, but Mei's revelation bothered her. She had wanted to rush in and shake Luce awake, but it would keep until morning. Now she needed to get out of bed, worried that her constant tossing would wake Luce. She gently rolled over, but she needn't worry. Luce wasn't in bed. Looking around, she didn't see her lover anywhere in the bedroom, and the bathroom was dark as well. She wasn't surprised. While Brooke was an early bird, Luce epitomized the night-owl concept, coming to bed late and rising early. Brooke had often told her that burning both ends off the candle would catch up to her eventually. Luce always responded, "I'll sleep when I'm dead." That, hopefully, wouldn't be for decades to come.

Easing out of bed, she slipped her robe on and grimaced as her thigh ached. She popped some pain relief, swallowed them down with a gulp of water, and went in search of Luce.

Light flickered underneath Luce's study door. Most likely Luce had opted for a stiff drink to calm her mind rather than burden Brooke with her problems. She'd probably find Luce asleep on the couch. After pushing the door open gently, she saw Luce sitting up, a circle of smoke crowning her head.

"Luce?"

"Brooke," Luce said, turning away from the TV. "What are you doing here? You should be resting."

"I was until I reached for you. Why don't you come to bed?"

"In a minute. Come here." Luce patted the couch and returned her attention to the TV.

Brooke saw someone in the pool. "Who's swimming at this hour?"

"Mei."

"Mei?"

"Uh-huh. Check this out." Luce pointed to the screen.

Brooke snuggled up beside Luce and rested her head on Luce's shoulder. Luce wrapped her arm around Brooke and pulled her close.

"Are you a Peeping Tom, now?"

"As a matter of fact, yes." Luce nodded toward the screen. "Do you see anything suspicious?"

"Luce—"

"Just look the next time she laps the pool."

They both stared at the screen, and as Mei swam in the opposite direction, the hidden tattoo resurfaced.

"What's that?"

"That's what I'd like to know." Luce hit the pause button, and the image filled the screen. "I can't make it out."

Brooke got up and walked to the screen for a closer look. "It seems to be writing of some type, or a..." Brooke traced the image with her finger, at a loss to describe what she was seeing. "I don't understand. What does it mean?"

"I think it's the missing piece that Mr. Horiyama at the tattoo studio was talking about."

"Wow, that's strange, don't you think?"

"I don't know what I think. But I do think she's not telling us everything."

"Maybe she doesn't know?" Brooke sat back down next to Luce. "I mean, it's on her back. How would she know what was put on there if you can't see it? How did you spot it?"

"The fluorescent lights in the pool area lit it up like a neon light."

"Wow, I mean...well, I don't know what I mean. Just wow."

"Now do you believe me? Something's not right here, and just a few minutes ago she was trying to chat up Sasha. She was almost flirting with Sasha. Now why would she act like that with someone who's guarding her and be standoffish with me?"

Brooke shook her head. She'd learned to trust Luce's judgment when it came to people. No, she didn't have any answers.

"Is there any way to get a picture of that, the tattoo, I mean?"

"Yeah. I froze the footage and snapped a picture of it on my phone. It's not very clear, and I don't think she's going to let me anywhere near it again."

"Maybe I can help."

"How?"

"I don't know. Maybe she'll talk to me like she did earlier tonight?"

"No. I don't want you involved, Brooke." Luce turned the TV off and hugged Brooke closer to her. "I've put you in enough danger. I'm not going to do that again. Wait, what do you mean she talked to you tonight? What did she say?"

Brooke sat up, faced Luce, then crossed and tucked her legs up under her.

"What's going on?" Luce asked, squinting her eyes like she did when she was suspicious.

"You know that photo album you have?"

"Yes."

"Well, I brought Mei in here and showed her around. Then we sat down and looked at the photos."

"And?"

"Well...I showed her a picture of your grandparents, and then I turned to the next page, and there we saw a picture of your mom and dad—"

"She jumped on that," Luce blurted out.

"Not exactly."

"What do you mean, not exactly?"

"I thought it was odd she didn't say something like, 'Oh, look, there's my father,' or 'Wow, my dad's young in this photo. Who's the woman he's with?' Nothing like that. In fact, she turned the page."

"Okay." Luce's sharp tone confirmed Brooke's hunch that she was definitely suspicious.

"We got to the photo of your grandfather with his kimono on and all of the Yakuza family standing around him..."

"Yeah."

"And she said, 'There's my dad.'" Brooke stood and walked over to the photo album and opened it to the photograph. Pointing to Frank, she showed Luce. "She says this is her dad."

"Are you kidding me?"

"Not according to Mei. Frank's her father."

Relief flooded Luce. She knew JP was dead. His pinkie finger, with his signet ring, had been sent to Frank, accompanied by a note from her grandfather.

"But how did she come by the green eyes, and you have to admit she does resemble me." Suddenly

Luce found herself defending the woman who had presented herself as her sister.

"Do a DNA test. There has to be an explanation for all of this," Brooke said, pointing to the TV. Mei was still doing laps.

"She said her mother's family had been paid off. Maybe Frank found out JP had another daughter and kept that knowledge in his back pocket, for use sometime in the future. His trump card, so to speak," Luce said, trying to make puzzle pieces fit that didn't belong where they were placed.

"Well, she thinks Frank is your father. Maybe we should just let that little piece of information stay tucked away until we figure out what to do with it."

"We?"

"I'm the one who found out about Frank being her father."

"True, but I still don't want you in the picture. If this involves Frank and that tattoo, it's more serious than we thought."

"He's sending me a message. Grandfather had someone deliver JP's pinkie to Frank in a box, with a note telling him he was going to exact revenge." Luce ran her hand down Brooke's arm, her body begging for Brooke's touch. "Frank knows that threat didn't die with my grandfather. It's just unfinished business that carries down to the next in line, and after what Frank did to you, I'm going to make good on the promise."

Brooke snuggled closer to Luce, letting the photo album fall between them. She hugged Luce tighter. "When will all of this end and we can return to our regular lives?"

"I don't know, lover." Luce kissed Brooke's cheek. "You can go back to work at *The Financial*

Times as soon as you feel better. I hear your boss is pretty understanding."

"Lloyd is. He's such a wonderful boss. I just love him." Brooke smiled.

Luce leaned back and gave Brooke a sideways glance. "I'm talking about the new boss. I hear she's the understanding one."

"Oh, you mean the new owner of *The Financial Times*. Meh, she's okay." Brooke giggled. Luce had purchased the magazine months ago in an effort to get closer to Brooke, and now she was officially a silent partner in the operation.

Brooke looked at the TV screen, watching Mei swim. She changed the subject. "If I can get her to let me look at the tattoo, maybe I can—"

"No, absolutely not." Luce stood and emptied her ashtray into the tin can she saved for her dead cigars and put her glass on the bar. "Let's go to bed. I need to think on this."

"But—"

"No. That's final." Luce grabbed Brooke's hand and helped her to her feet.

Brooke didn't like being shut out like this, but she wasn't exactly in any condition to argue the point at the moment. She'd have to come up with a way to help Luce without involving her. Shuffling back to the room, she closed and locked the door behind them. Brooke could see that Luce was oblivious to everything around her, as she was clearly thinking about Mei's hidden tattoo.

Reaching around Luce, Brooke tugged on the edge of the sweater and pulled it up and over Luce's head. Luce started to turn around, but Brooke stopped her. Brooke ran her fingers under the band of her black bra and pushed them around back. A quick pass of a nipple made Luce gasp. Unsnapping the bra, Brooke let it fall to the floor. She wrapped her arms around Luce and held her body to her own front. Luce's scent wafted to Brooke's nose. She'd know that perfume mixed with soap anywhere. She often cuddled Luce's pillows, in hopes of catching a whiff of Luce that might have lingered. Did all lovers do that? She caressed the soft hip of her lover before sliding up the slight curve to her breast.

"Brooke."

"Relax. I just want to touch you. It's been weeks since we've been alone, and I miss you…the way your body feels under my fingers. The way it reacts to a simple touch." Brooke slipped her hand around to the front and flicked the first button of Luce's jeans open. Sliding her hand down, she eased into the silky front of Luce's panties. "Haven't you missed me?"

Luce stilled Brooke's hands and dropped her head. "You have no idea."

Slipping past Luce's grasp and moving farther down into her pants, she said, "Oh, I think I do." Then Brooke darted her tongue out to trace a line from Luce's shoulder to her ear lobe. Brooke gently bit the lobe and then blew a seductive warm breath into Luce's ear.

Chapter Sixteen

Brooke stretched and reached for Luce, again. Gone.

This was becoming a habit that Brooke was going to have to break Luce of. As she looked at the clock, it blinked back seven thirty. Luce was probably working the Frank angle already, if Brooke knew her.

A quick sponge bath, some sweats, and she walked down the study to catch Luce before she made an excuse to go to the office. Instead, she found Sasha standing guard in the office, Mei on the couch thumbing through the photo album, but no Luce.

"Where's Luce?"

"She said to tell you she stepped out to pick up a few things. She'll be home to have lunch with you and her," Sasha said, clearly pissed and tossing her chin in Mei's direction.

"You're mad 'cause you have to watch her?" Brooke said, rubbing her hand up and down Sasha's upper arm, a show of support for the woman's predicament.

"I'd rather push needles into my eye than be a babysitter."

"How about I sit with Mei, and you can relax for an hour or so," Brooke offered.

"The oyabun wouldn't like that."

Brooke raised her eyebrows and frowned, feeling her forehead furrow. "I think I can handle the oyabun.

Go…" Brooke pushed Sasha's stout frame through the door. "Shoo. I'll entertain Mei."

"But—"

"Do you want me to tell the oyabun that you disobeyed a direct order from me? By the time she asks you what demand you disobeyed, it'll be too late to cool her temper."

"True, but I just want to go on record that I'm leaving against my will."

"Dually noted. Now shoo." Brooke closed the door behind Sasha and walked over to the couch. "Do you mind if I sit?"

"Please," Mei said, bowing. "I am guest in your home."

"You're family, Mei. Not a guest. I hope you'll make yourself comfortable"

"That is very kind of you. Thank you."

"So, I see you're looking at the photo album again."

"Yes. I hope it's okay? I wanted to see if there were more photos of my father."

"Of course. Did you find others?"

"Yes." Mei's fingers were stuck between several pages in the album. "Here." She showed Brooke. "And here and here."

Brooke hadn't realized there were so many photos of Frank with the oyabun, but he was Tamiko's second-in-command, so it was plausible, if Luce's grandfather was in them. As his second, he was responsible for Tamiko's safety.

"I see. Would you like me to ask if Luce will allow us to make copies of them?"

"Oh." Mei perked up. "Do you think sister would allow that?"

"I'm sure she would." Brooke held her hands out for the album. "Why don't we take the photos out and stack them on her desk, and when she gets back from running errands, we can inquire."

"Oh, yes. Thank you." Mei's eyes were brimming with tears.

"Why the tears?"

"Father never let me take pictures of him. I have no photos of us together. So, this is special to me." Mei held her hand over her heart.

Mei's naïveté regarding Frank was sad. Once she found out that he was a killer and probably not her father, Brooke suspected it would crush her. Frank didn't deserve the respect Mei had for him. The way Mei talked lovingly about Frank was almost quite profound.

"What do you say we go get some lunch? Celeste is a wonderful cook."

"Yes, of course. Can I have a…" Mei put her finger to her lips and tapped them, thinking. "A…one of those pieces of meat with bread?"

"A hamburger?" Brooke asked.

"Yes, I believe that is what they are called, and a drink that fizzes."

"A soda?"

"Yes."

"How about some fries?"

"Oh, are those good?"

"Come on. We can have an early lunch. Celeste makes the best burgers."

༄༅༄༅

Brooke checked her watch for the fiftieth time

that afternoon. Luce still hadn't returned home and wasn't answering her phone. She knew Luce was a big girl and could take care of herself, but with Petrov and Frank still out there, she was worried.

Hunting down Sasha, who was standing guard outside Mei's bedroom, she asked if she'd heard anything.

"Any word from Luce?"

"Not yet, ma'am."

"Did anyone go out with her?"

"No, ma'am. Why?"

"Well, it's getting late and I've tried her cell phone, but she's not answering."

"I'll call Momo and see if he's heard anything."

"Thank you."

"Of course," Sasha said, pulling out her phone. A quick conversation between the two didn't sound promising. "Boss was supposed to meet him at the office for instructions on finding Frank, but she hasn't showed up."

"Tell Momo to come here. I'm worried. It isn't like her to not show up for an appointment or answer her phone."

"Yes, ma'am." Sasha was stern in her response to Momo. "He's on his way. I should call Sammy. He'll want to know what's happening."

"Yes. I think he needs to be informed. I'm sure he has his hands full with those two women."

"I'm sure," Sasha said.

"When Momo gets here, let me know. We'll meet in Luce's study."

"Yes, ma'am."

Brooke walked back to their bedroom and grabbed her phone, trying Luce one more time. If she didn't pick up, Brooke definitely knew something was wrong. It went right to voice mail. What now? Maybe she should call Colby. This just wasn't like Luce. Opening up her contact list on her phone, she dialed the navigation system in the SUV. Maybe she was driving and couldn't answer. The phone rang through and went to voice mail again.

Shit. This was bad on so many levels.

After punching another number, she waited as it rang.

"Brookie, what can I do for you? Are you glad to be out of the hospital?"

"Colby, Luce is missing." Brooke's hand trembled as she said the words. "I don't know what to do."

※※※※

Brooke limped to the door. She wanted to be the one to talk to Colby while the others waited in Luce's study.

"Hey," Brooke said, accepting a hug from her ex.

"Hey. Any word yet?"

"No. Not a whisper." Brooke moved aside and swept her hand in a welcoming motion, allowing Colby to enter. Colby was dressed in her "office drag," as she always referred to it.

"Hmm," Colby said, stepping past Brooke. "Where are the rest of the kids?"

Brooke nodded toward the study. "Back there. They're waiting for us. Sammy came back, and Sasha is staying with Mrs. Petrov and Katarina."

Colby stopped cold, causing Brooke to bump into her. "What do you mean, 'Sasha is with Mrs. Petrov and Katarina?'"

Oh, shit. Had she actually just said that? Fuck.

Brooke walked around Colby, but not before Colby grabbed her arm and stopped her. "What's going on?"

"Luce didn't tell you?"

"No. I guess she left out that little nugget of information when she called me to run interference for her yesterday."

"I'm sorry, Colby. She told me yesterday. I don't think she wanted to get you involved in her issues with Petrov."

"Really? Well, she had no problem involving me yesterday."

Brooke touched Colby's arm and stopped her from stomping away. "You can have that conversation with her when we find her, but right now, she's missing, and I'm scared."

"I'm not going to sugarcoat this, Brooke. You should be. She's messing with the Russian mafia, and they aren't nice people. We've been turning up dead girls all over town, and the drug trade and human trafficking are booming because of Petrov. So, she's a liability to them because of her attitude toward drugs and trafficking. They're going to kill her if she has Petrov's wife and daughter."

"I know." Brooke broke down and started crying. She couldn't help herself. Colby stating the obvious only reinforced Brooke's worst fear. If they didn't find her, Luce would be dead.

"The only card Luce has to play right now is having those women, and if I know Luce, she's not going to tell him anything. Not without getting something back."

"I hope you're right, because we don't have

anything on Luce's whereabouts. I've called the local police and put a BOLO out on her. If they see her, they'll pick her up."

"BOLO?"

"Be on the lookout."

"But what if they arrest her?"

Colby glanced sideways at Brooke. "Trust me, if they arrest her, she'll be a lot safer with them than wherever she is right now."

Chapter Seventeen

Two days ago

Luce heard Petrov push through the door. Her daily beating was arriving. She ignored his spouting of Russian bravado that always irritated her. She wished he'd just knock her around and then leave her alone. She was sure he figured that if he softened her up, her lips would spill the whereabouts of his wife and daughter. Fat chance.

He stood a better chance of choking on his own bullshit.

"Back for another round?" she spit out.

"You are the loveliest punch bag I've ever had, Luce Potter. Why don't you just make it easier on yourself? Tell me where my wife and daughter are, and I promise to make death quick."

"Fuck you."

"You want Petrov? I can make arrangements for shower and pokey, pokey," he said, thrusting his hips in her face.

"I'd rather eat a bullet."

"Ah, that reminds me." He picked up the revolver and spun the cylinder. The chrome had his fingerprints all over it, but it still shone. "This is very nice gun, don't you think? I think your father had one exactly like it. Do you know how I know?" He flashed it in front of her face. "Because I gave it to John Wayne. I mean JP. He was always cowboy, you know?"

Luce didn't say anything. If he was going to shoot her, she wished he'd get it over with so she didn't have to listen to his bullshit.

He picked up the single bullet from the coffee table in front of her and slid it into one of the chambers. Flicked his wrist, closing the revolver, then gave it a quick spin.

Tick, tick, tick.

The cylinder stopped.

Petrov pushed the muzzle against her forehead this time. The first click of the hammer echoed in the room.

"Have anything to say, Potter?"

Luce pushed her head against the muzzle, forcing his hand back an inch.

"Okay."

Another click as the hammer was pulled and ready for action.

"You sure?" Petrov toyed with Luce as he pulled it from her head.

She looked straight ahead at the dirty curtains. Sad. Those would be the last things she would see on this side of the dirt.

"Have it your way." He bent down and whispered in her ear. "I'm going to find Brooke and fuck her brains out, and then I'm going to make her work for me in one of my whorehouses. When she can no longer fuck, I'm going to make her into a junkie. Your girlfriend will be my bitch."

"You bastard," she said, turning toward him just as he raised the gun and pulled the trigger.

Pop.

Chapter Eighteen

Brooke hadn't slept in days. Her mind ran different scenarios for Luce's disappearance, but not one of them included Luce just walking away. Brooke feared the worst—her lover lying in a ditch dead. The possibilities were endless.

"Ms. Erickson, Agent Water is here. Would you like me to put her in the study?"

Brooke jerked at the sudden intrusion. Colby showing up meant bad news, she just knew it. Her heart raced, her palms were sweating, and her mind ran an endless loop of Luce hurt somewhere without her. Was she even still alive? Of course she was. She couldn't let herself think that way.

"Ms. Erickson?"

"Yes, Celeste. Please show Agent Water to the study." Brooke wiped her eyes. "Celeste, is she alone?"

"Yes, ma'am."

A sliver of hope and relief coursed through Brooke. "Thank you, Celeste. I'll be right there."

"Yes, ma'am."

Looking in the mirror at her disheveled appearance reflected back the inner turmoil Brooke was carrying around. Luce had never left Brooke unless they had words, heated or otherwise. So this was tearing her up inside. The comb snagged on a few tangles as she ripped it through her hair. Pain might be more comforting than words of endearment from the staff, or from Colby. Rubbing the washrag across her face, she tried to perk up.

For what?

Unless Colby had good news for her, there wasn't much use making herself presentable. Her body ached still from the attack at Frank's hands. Her mind was just starting to get back on working rails. John Lloyd had called to check in and find out when she thought she might come back to work, on light duty. Then this.

It had been almost two days since she saw Luce.

Two days. Two Fucking Days.

Brooke stepped into the hallway, composed herself, and walked down to the study. Sammy was sitting across from Colby. They'd been chatting about something, but when she walked in, they stopped.

He stood and bowed. "Ms. Erickson."

"Hi, Sammy."

"You're looking well."

"Liar," she said. "Surely you jest."

Brooke sat on the couch next to Sammy and patted his leg. Worry creased his forehead, and he offered a limp smile.

"Agent Water. What's the news?"

She noticed Colby give a sigh before she answered. Not good news.

"We found Luce's car." She paused. "It was down on Main Street." Colby tugged on her ear, a sign Brooke recognized. She always pulled or scratched her ear when she was nervous.

"And?" Brooke braced herself.

"It's down at the forensic lab. We're going over it right now."

"And?"

"We haven't found any blood or anything that

would make us suspicious, yet. If that's what you're asking. However..."

Brooke closed her eyes and buried her head in her hands. Sammy gently touched her back and tried to be as comforting as he could, considering the boundaries that were in place between the wife of the oyabun and her second-in-command.

"Her phone and her gun were in the center console."

Sammy piped up. "No signs of a struggle?"

Colby looked between her and Sammy. "We found scuff marks on the SUV."

"Like someone hit her?" Brooke asked.

"No. More like shoe leather. A partial imprint from a shoe was on the rear passenger door."

"Oh, then she's alive, right?"

"Brooke..."

She threw up her hands. "Don't, Colby. I'm not even going to entertain the fact that she might be dead. I just won't. Now what else do you have?"

Colby shook her head. "That's all. We're looking at why she might have been downtown and why she would have her phone with her. Got any ideas?"

Brooke shook her head. She didn't.

"Sammy?"

"What's around the area of her car?"

"Coffee shop, there's a small organic market, a flower shop—"

"Full Blossoms, or something like that," Colby said, looking through her note pad. "Blossoms."

Brooke noticed Sammy didn't say anything. He just pursed his lips together and pulled out his phone. Tapping the screen, he studied the phone for a minute and then said, "That's where the oyabun get flowers for Ms. Erickson." He turned the phone around and flashed the screen at Colby. It was a text for him to pick up a delivery, days ago.

"Okay, so she was going to the flower store, maybe?"

"Maybe," Sammy said.

"Did anyone see anything? It was broad daylight, for God's sake." Brooke's voice was wavering.

"We do have someone who thinks they saw something. Another SUV pulled up to a car. Two guys slipped out and put a black bag or jacket over a person's head and shoved them into the SUV."

"That's Luce. Then she's alive. I'll wager Petrov's behind this."

"Brooke, calm down. We don't know that for sure."

Brooke stood, her hands on her hips. "But Luce kidnapped Petrov's wife and daughter. Surely he wants to use her to get them back. God, Colby, you don't have to be a special agent to figure that one out."

Brooke started to pace behind the couch.

"Brooke, we don't know that for sure."

"You already said that, Colby. So tell me. What are you doing to find her?"

"I'm working with the local authorities. We're looking through some security footage from one of the businesses that had a camera positioned to see out the front window. If we're lucky, we can get something off the tape."

"Okay. What else?" Brooke crossed her arms and stared at Colby. At least this was hopeful news.

Luce was a survivor, and she wasn't one to give up, so Brooke shouldn't either. She knew Luce would do whatever it took to get home to her. Even if it meant she had to make a few life-or-death decisions to get away.

"We're doing everything we can. I just stopped by to give you an update."

Brooke softened her tone. "Thanks, Colby. I'm sorry. I'm just frantic. I'm sure you can understand."

"I do, and now is where I get to tell you to let us do our job. Don't be going off and trying to find her, Brooke. Petrov's a dangerous man, and as you said, Luce has his wife and daughter. He's like a caged dog, with very few options. So...if you hear anything, either of you, call me immediately. Don't try to find him or take him down. You might inadvertently get Luce killed. Understand?"

"Yes," they both said in unison.

"Good. I'll keep you posted. Remember, if you hear anything, call me." Colby held her finger and thumb, in the shape of a phone, to her ear.

"I'll walk you out, Agent Water," Sammy said.

"No bother. I know my way out by now. Brooke..." Colby leaned down and gave Brooke a brief hug. "I'll call later and check up on you."

"Thanks." Brooke barely returned the hug. Her mind was already spinning with a plan.

As soon as the door shut, Brooke stood, pulled the phone book from the bookcase, and thumbed through to the yellow pages. "She said Blossom, right?"

"Ms. Erickson—"

"You don't expect me to sit here while Luce is in trouble, do you?"

"But, Ms. Erickson."

"Get Momo. I think you need to pay a visit to the stores around there. Someone saw something. Main Street is too busy for a kidnapping to get noticed. Hell, everyone has their cell phones out. Someone could have caught it all on their phone."

"Ms. Erickson, please."

Brooke shot him a terse look. "Fine. I can do this without you. I'll let the oyabun know how helpful you've been."

"I'll call Momo," he said, clearly defeated.

Brooke didn't want to strong-arm Sammy, but she wasn't about to sit around and do nothing.

"Thank you. Now let's come up with a plan to find the oyabun," she said, pulling paper and pen over to the phone book.

Chapter Nineteen

Present day

Luce dropped her head to her chest. Her guts were killing her, and all she wanted to do was pee. An escape plan right about now would be excellent, because the next time someone came into the room, she swore she was going to die.

The door swung open and hit the wall with a crash. A hole in the wall was its reward for being in the wrong place at the wrong time.

"Luce. Your lucky day. It's Ivan, to take you to pee." He thumped his chest and quirked his eyebrows.

Why were these men always trying to come on to themselves, 'cause clearly their moves were lost on her?

"Where's Frank?"

"Frank?" Ivan gave Luce a confused look, and then reality hit him. "Oh, Asian dude who fucked your friend up," Ivan deadpanned and then whispered, "Did he kill her?"

"What do you think?"

"Yeah. I don't like that slanty-eyed bastard. He's bad news. Sucks boss's ass all the time. Said he got plan for you. Something about daughter."

"Mei?"

"Meh. I don't know name. I try not to pay attention to talking asshole. Really pain in ass. You know what I mean?" Ivan slapped her shoulder, then clapped his hands together. "Okay, so you dodge bullet again. Hey, that's pretty good. Petrov pissed, but who cares, right?"

"Right," Luce said, going along with the overly friendly enemy.

"Okay you get to have shower and use the real toilet."

"Finally."

"If you're good, I mean really good, I'll wash your back."

"Really? I'm good. How about you just let me get this grime off me, and we can talk later. Besides, it's that time of the month and I have a headache."

"Jesus, do all you women have headache when you get cycle? My wife same way. She cramps and cries like infant." He grabbed his head, covering his ears, and waved his head back and forth. "I can't stand crying. I want to take a knife and stab my eyes out."

Luce corrected him. "Don't you mean ears?"

"Whatever."

Luce wished she could feel sorry for the bastard, but the longer his rant went on, the less likely she'd be able to have enough time to put her plan into action. "Bathroom, please."

"Yeah, yeah." He reached down to uncuff her one hand and then recuffed it as he brought them together. Lifting her arms up, he bent her over and walked her to the bathroom. Ivan unlocked the cuff and attached her to the shower rod.

"Hey, how am I supposed to go to the bathroom with my hand cuffed up here? I guess you'll have to wipe my ass, Ivan." Luce didn't bother to look at the man. She knew what she'd said would punch his buttons, especially since she was on her period.

His face dropped close to hers as he started to turn her around, shoving her toward the shower. "I don't wipe my bedridden mama's ass. What make you think I'd like yours?"

"Well, I can't go to the bathroom in the shower, now can I?"

His gaze roamed over her body. It was obvious what he was thinking, but he wasn't about to see her naked.

"Let me go to the bathroom, and then I'll strip and get in the shower."

"Why not? You can't beat the bullet one more day. Besides, Ivan likes a beautiful woman. I would hate to see all go to waste."

Luce wanted to remove the sick smile from his lips as he wet them, leering at her.

Patience, she told herself. If she got her way, she'd do more than just wipe the grin off the fucking lecherous bastard's face.

Ivan closed one cuff so tight it was practically cutting off the blood to her hand. After opening the other, he snapped it to the towel bar behind the toilet.

"Seriously?" Luce hissed out.

He shoved her backward onto the toilet. "Make it work." He then took up a position against the door, leaning against the frame as he waited.

She unsnapped her slacks before she looked up at him again.

Ivan smirked and raised his hand, the cuff key dangling from his finger. "You can piss in bucket."

Luce made a show of looking around the room. "Where am I going to go? Use my superpowers, shrink, and escape through the fan vent?"

"Ivan," someone screamed from another room.

"I guess you get your wish." He smiled, wagging his finger at her as he admonished her. "Don't go anywhere. Ivan will be right back to scrub you all over."

The door slammed, and then she heard a key being shoved into the old skeleton lock, the brass grinding as it locked.

Luce stood, grabbed the towel bar with both hands, and strained to dislodge it from the wall. Jerking back and forth on it, she finally pried one end loose and slipped a cuff off. She only had minutes to put her plan into motion before Ivan, or someone else, came in to retrieve her.

Wrapping her hand in a towel, she hit the mirror, barely making a sound as the glass broke. Pulling a shard from it, she inspected it to make sure it was long enough. What she did next would never leave that room. Luce reached down and covered her hands in blood, using it to spread all over face, neck, and hands. She lay motionless on the floor. She would have to be convincing if she was going to pull this off. When the door was flung open, Ivan found Luce sprawled on the floor, blood covering the shard in her hand and her neck.

Without hesitating, he ran over to Luce, falling to his knees and turning her over.

"You crazy bitch. Boss is going to kill me now."

Before he could say another word, Luce let the momentum of her body being flipped over help her thrust the shard of glass into his throat. Blood swirled from his mouth, and he reached for the shard sticking out of his neck. She shoved the towel into his mouth, pushed him back against the wall, and straddled his flailing body. Using the open end of the cuff, she pounded it with her fist into his temple. He writhed for a moment, then went limp against the wall, his eyes open, staring at her.

"Christ."

A marathon would've been easier to finish, she thought as she pushed herself off the floor and fished through his pockets. She rolled her bruised wrist out of the cuff, leaving the protruding end embedded in his head. Still unsteady on her feet, she turned the shower on and pulled Ivan into the hot spray. It would buy her some time if his buddies thought he was in here playing peekaboo with the hostage.

Reaching for the washcloth hanging in the shower, she wiped the blood from her neck, hands, and face. After she rinsed it, she wiped down the wall. Why? She wasn't sure, but she did it anyway.

Searching through the cabinets, she found another washrag, folded it into thirds, and shoved it into her underwear. Her personal hygiene would have to wait. Her life was at stake, and she needed to bolt while the adrenaline rush was still surging.

Peeking around the door, she made sure the room was clear, then closed the bathroom door and locked it behind her. As she peered down the hall, she couldn't see anyone. Sliding against the wall, she closed the bedroom door and slowly locked herself in the room.

She moved as fast as she could and snatched the gun, shoved the single bullet into the chamber, and slid the gun into her waistband. She looked at the chair again, wishing she could take a moment to catch her breath. But laughter down the hall reminded her why she couldn't rest. She pushed the curtains aside and looked out the window. Dusk was edging in, and she was on the second floor. A long drop, but it wouldn't kill her. Opening the window, she took her first breath of fresh air. Because of where she'd been cuffed, Petrov hadn't taken any precautions in securing the window.

His first mistake.

Pushing as hard as she could muster her tired muscles, she slowly eased the window up just enough to slip out onto the ledge. It was barely wide enough to get a foothold, but she managed. Luce pulled the curtains closed and the window shut. A man walked below her in the alleyway with a big bag of garbage, tossing it into a dumpster and leaving the lid open, then went back inside. It was only a few feet to her right. Could she hit it? She had to. Her life depended on it, and then her motivation sounded behind her. Someone was banging on the bedroom door.

Launching herself toward the dumpster, she landed inside, but not before her foot made contact with the edge.

Crack.

Without thinking, she pulled some garbage on top of her just as someone swung the curtains above her wide.

"Check the bathroom. I bet Ivan's in there fucking that bitch."

Peeking through the debris, she watched the man walk away from the window. She only had seconds before they found Ivan dead. Easing over the edge of the dumpster, she landed on her feet and buckled. Her left foot was broken.

Pushing the pain from her mind, she hugged the wall and looked around. A grimy brick wall was at one end of the alley, the street with bustling traffic at the other end. Several doors emptied into the alley, but they weren't offering refuge. Russians owned this part of town. They'd taken it over when the economy started to tank, seeing an opportunity to run their human trafficking. It was easier to smuggle women into shipping containers and run their prostitution rings out of the filthy boxes. When they were done, they literally took them out to sea and sank them. She was in their territory, and now what was she going to do? Patting her stomach, she felt the revolver stuck in her waistband.

One bullet.

Chapter Twenty

Brooke sat staring at her cell phone on the coffee table and the landline next to it. Both felt more like a lifeline than anything. Colby said she'd call if she had any news. Sammy said he'd call if he found anything out. So far, no one was calling. Maybe she needed to phone Maggie and ask her to prescribe something for her anxiety. She was practically crawling the walls. Grabbing the TV controller, she hit the security link and looked around the house.

Great. Now she was paranoid, too. Well, when life gave you lemons, make a lemon-drop martini. Flipping cameras, she watched the outside cameras. As she scouted the gardens, she watched the gardener mow the grass, clip the Japanese boxwoods, deadhead the flowers, and trim Luce's prizes roses she'd inherited from her mother and grandmother. The cherry blossoms were starting to bloom. Their smell and beauty would soon fill the house with buds and clippings. God, she hoped Luce would be home soon to see how lovely they were.

Of course she would, Brooke told herself.

Switching to another channel, Brooke spotted Mei, swimming again. The woman was part fish. She lapped the pool several times before she pulled up to the side and caught her breath. Mei looked up at the camera, her expression vacant. Hoisting herself up to sit on the side of the pool, she positioned her back to the camera, reached for her towel, and patted her face.

Brooke could see the highlighted tattoo perfectly now. It entwined with the vibrant colors—the blacks, blues, reds, and greens that made up the dragon. Looking closer, Brooke could see another message written in fluorescent white. Zooming in, she snapped the clearest picture of the message yet. She wouldn't be able to translate whatever this was, but she knew who would.

Auntie.

※※※※

"Sammy, I want you to take me to Auntie's when you get back."

"Ms. Erickson?"

"When will you be home?"

"We're almost done looking for witnesses."

"Any luck?"

"I think so. I'll bring home what I find out so you can see."

"Maybe we should call Agent Water?"

"I don't think that's a good idea. They won't talk to her, Ms. Erickson. That is why she is still coming up empty. If you get my meaning."

"I do."

The shops where Sammy was fishing weren't exactly federal-agent friendly. Now, family, aka Yakuza friendly, that was different. Luce had a reputation that closed as many doors as it opened. No one down on Main Street wanted to get on the oyabun's bad side. So, Brooke imagined, Sammy had a way of opening lips and greasing palms.

"How much longer?"

"About ten minutes. I'm finishing up with the gallery across from Blossom."

"Okay. I'll see you in a few."

Brooke turned her attention to the security camera and watched Mei. Perhaps she needed to have a conversation with Luce's sister again.

Opening the door to the poolroom, Brooke nodded to Sasha, who looked so bored Brooke was glad to relieve the poor woman.

"Why don't you go grab something to eat? I want to talk to Mei."

"But Boss said—"

"Boss isn't here, and Sammy will be back in a few minutes. I want to have a meeting when he gets here, so go eat."

"But—"

"I said, go." Brooke pushed Sasha toward the door.

Turning around, she slipped her flip-flops off, rolled her sweats up, and sat on the edge of the pool dangling her feet in the warm saline water. God, she just wanted to jump in and relax. Her wound looked better each day, and she suspected her next doctor's appointment would clear her for a shower. Until then, she'd try to be a good patient.

"Hello," Mei said, gliding through the water toward Brooke. "How do you feel?"

"I'm okay. How about you?"

"Okay. Any news on my sister?"

Brooke shook her head. "Nothing yet."

"I'm sure sister will be okay, yes?"

"I'm sure."

"Do you swim?"

"I love to swim, but I can't just yet." Brooke

tapped her thigh.

"I could take a look if you like. I know ancient medicine. Perhaps I could offer some remedies that would help?"

"Really?"

"Yes. I'm trained in the healing arts. Herbs and potions for healthy body."

"Oh. I didn't know that. Where did you learn?"

"I went to school for Oriental medicine."

"Well, you're just full of surprises, aren't you?" Brooke splashed her feet in the pool.

"For example, this is salt water, very good for the skin and can pull negative energy and toxins out of the body. Perhaps you should get in?"

"I'm under doctor's orders not to."

"Western medicine is so toxic sometimes. They forget that herbs and oils were the first things used to heal the body."

"Yes. Sometimes the old stuff is better."

"I give you a reiki massage, hot stones on your chakras. It will realign your chi." Mei moved her hands along Brooke's legs, drawing her hands toward her. The heat from her hands almost had a relaxing feel to them.

"You pull the energy toward the injured part of the body to aid in healing," she said.

"Perhaps later."

"I promise I will not hurt."

"I believe you," Brooke said. She didn't want to hurt Mei's feelings, but, like Luce, she wasn't sure about the woman's motives. A massage sounded wonderful, though.

"So Mei, how have you liked being in the United States?"

"Well, I must be honest and say I haven't seen much of it."

"I know. I'm sorry. Once Luce gets back and we can figure out what's going on, perhaps we can do some touristy stuff."

"Touristy stuff?" she said, treading water away from Brooke.

"See the sights around town and up the coast. It's beautiful at the beach."

"We have beach in Japan."

"I'm sure you do. Mei, can I ask you a question?"

"Of course."

"What was your father like?"

"My father?" Mei gave Brooke a confused look. "He was not around much."

"So who took care of you?"

Mei looked at Brooke and then swam across the pool, leaving Brooke to wonder if she'd pried too much.

On her next lap, Mei stopped and rested on the edge of the pool. "My second mother. Jujem."

"What's she like?"

"She is very nice. I miss her, very much." Mei looked at Brooke. "Is your mother alive?"

"She is, but we don't speak often."

"And your father?"

"He's alive, too. They live in another state, so it makes it hard to see them as much as I would like."

"Did they not come to visit when you were in hospital?"

"They wanted to, but I told them to wait until I was home. I didn't want them to see me like this."

"Hmm. Yes, it would be hard to have a daughter so ill."

"That's right. I wanted to spare them and myself

all the questions. I'm just not ready for that."

"Do they not approve of Luce?"

"Hmm, well, it's not an issue. They don't have a choice. It's my life."

"Oh, it would not be accepted in my family."

"Really." Brooke looked at Mei. "What about Luce?"

"Hmm." Mei had a surprised look on her face. "I had not thought about sister."

"What was your childhood like, Mei?"

Mei looked quizzically at Brooke and then backstroked away from her.

Obviously, Mei was avoiding her, but she needed something to take her mind off Luce. Her insides were churning, her nerves were firing, and her mind was jumbled with thoughts of Luce dead.

Diversion.

She needed to stop thinking, so perhaps she could find out about Mei.

"I'd like to hear what your childhood was like."

"I was a gentle child. My father says my feeling were hurt easily. That I should be stronger. So…I tried to be stronger, and I picked fights with the boys. They would pull my…how do you call hair that is weaved?"

"Pigtails?"

"Yes, those. They would pull my pigtails, and I would chase them and hit them."

"What did your mother say?"

"My father said I should be smarter."

"I don't understand. He said you needed to be stronger."

"He meant of the mind." Mei pointed to her head. "I let the boys beat me when I reacted. So, my father whipped me."

"He struck you?"

"He said that I should be able to handle pain efficiently. I should not react, but to be on the guard. Pay attention to my surroundings and understand that there are people who will hurt me."

"That's odd to tell a child. A child should learn what its boundaries are, be able to explore and make mistakes."

"Mistakes dishonor the family. Family honor is held above all else."

Brooke shook her head. She could hear Luce saying the exact same thing. "What did you do for fun?"

Mei pushed herself up onto the edge of the swimming pool and looked at Brooke. "What did you do for fun?" she asked, mimicking Brooke.

Brooke shrugged and then said, "Rode my bike and played with my friends, after school."

"Hmm."

"So what did you do for fun?" Brooke asked again.

"I went to school. Come home and do classwork. Help with house, then sleep."

"What about the weekends?"

"More school. Wash clothes. Work in garden."

"So you didn't do anything fun."

Mei shrugged. "I like to draw."

"Really. Do you have anything you can show me?"

Mei turned her shoulder and pointed to her back. "You drew that?"

"My father said, 'Mei, I want you to draw dragon, holding cherry blossoms and opening scroll.'"

"Then he made you get it tattooed on your back?" Brooke couldn't believe it. This had to be considered torture in the United States. What were acceptable practices in other cultures often surprised Brooke, but this took the cake. "It's stunning, Mei." Brooke had to admit that the artwork was amazing. She studied the tattoo closer. "May I look closer? It's beautiful."

"I was honored to represent my family. My father said one day it would save my life." Mei dropped her head and pushed a drop of water down her thigh, and then another.

Brooke grabbed her hand and squeezed. "It's okay. Family can be very powerful."

"I would never dishonor my father's request. He took care of me, and I owe him so much."

"Maybe," Brooke said, struggling to stand. "I'm feeling a little tired. Do you mind if I go to bed, Mei?"

Mei jumped to her feet, grabbed Brooke's hand, pulling her up, and bowed. "Of course. Would you like me to prepare your bed or pour your bath?"

Stunned by the request, Brooke grabbed Mei's shoulders and looked her in the eyes. "Here, Mei, you don't have to wait on anyone. You are free to do whatever you want."

"I am not allowed to leave," Mei reminded Brooke.

"If you'd like to go somewhere, just tell Sasha, and she has my permission to take you."

"That is very generous of you, Ms. Erickson." Mei bowed.

"When Luce gets back, we can sort all of this out. Okay?"

"Of course. Please sleep well, Ms. Erickson."

"Good night, Mei."

Brooke knew sleep would elude her, so she had something else up her sleeve. If Colby wouldn't tell her anything, she'd find someone who could.

Chapter Twenty-one

Luce's foot throbbed in her boot as she snaked her way around dumpsters and trashcans. Leaning against the wall, she peered around the corner of the old brick building. The brisk breeze blew crumpled paper and used coffee cups down the dirty sidewalk. Luce looked up, trying to get her bearings in the city. The old clock tower was to her right. And far off in the distance she could see the dock tower to her left and smell the warehouse that processed fish.

God, she was miles from home.

Cardboard boxes, shelters for the homeless, lined the wall to her left. A grizzled man edged his way out of one, looked at Luce, and nodded, shoving his hand out.

"Got a buck?" he asked, slurring his words and wobbling toward her.

Surprised, Luce patted her slacks and felt the folded-up bills in her slacks. Petrov hadn't searched her except to make sure she didn't have her phone. She'd left the damn thing in the SUV, like an idiot. Reaching in, she separated a bill from the stack and palmed it. "You got an extra blanket in there?"

"You got a buck?" He pointed to the makeshift squat. "I got something in there."

Luce handed him a hundred-dollar bill.

"Jesus, lady. You can have the whole thing for this." He snapped the bill tight. "Take whatever you want," he said, suddenly seeming sober.

"Thanks." Luce crawled inside the box and noticed how everything was in order. Clothes folded in neat stacks, shoes lined up against the wall, and his bedding rolled up and tied off.

"Hey, you see a woman come through here?"

Luce froze. Fuck. They'd found her.

"A lady?" the man repeated.

"Yeah, ass hat. Black slacks, white shirt. Did you see her come by?"

"Hmm. Saw somebody a minute ago. Ran past me like the devil was chasing her."

"Which way did she go?"

"I asked her for a buck, but she just kept going. I think she was ignoring me."

Which way did she go?"

Luce heard the poor guy being pushed up against the wall.

"Hey."

"Which way?"

"Toward town. Geez."

"You sure?"

"Look, buddy, she didn't give me a buck, so I just watched her ass run away. You got a buck?" Feet plodded off in the distance as Luce heard him say, "A man's gotta…assholes."

Luce slumped against the brick wall, pulling the revolver as the cardboard door jerked open. She pointed it directly at the head poking in.

"Hey, whoa." He put his hands up. "You better get moving. They might come back."

"Why did you do that?"

"You help me, so I help you. Over there, in that backpack, are some clothes. Can't vouch for how clean they are, but they're looking for you in those." He pointed at her own grungy mess.

"Thanks." Luce reached for what little the guy had. She felt guilty for taking this stuff, but he was right. They were looking for a beat-up, well-dressed Asian woman, not a homeless one.

A few minutes later she slipped out of the shelter looking anything but the polished businesswoman she was. Oversized pants and a flannel shirt covered her slim body. She'd shoved her stuff into the backpack and slung it over her shoulder, completing her homeless ensemble.

"Now you look different. Sorry I didn't have something better." He stared at her. "Oh, hey, you need to cover that hair. Here." He took off his baseball cap and handed it to her. It was a championship San Francisco Giants hat from last year's World Series.

"I can't take this," she said.

"I'll find another one." He smiled.

Luce reached into her pants, pulled out another hundred-dollar bill, and handed it to him. "Take this. It should cover your stuff."

"Nope. We're solid."

"Take it," she insisted. "What's your name?"

"Doug, but most people call me Tank."

"Thanks, Tank." Luce turned to leave but stopped. "Why did you help me?"

He offered a smile. "My mom always said to never hit a lady. You look like someone who was used as a punching bag, and I think those guys looking for you were the boxers. Am I right?"

Luce didn't look at him. She couldn't admit she'd let Petrov do this to her.

"Just promise me one thing..." he said.

"What's that?"

"You won't go back to the guy who did that to you." He pointed to her face.

"Oh, you don't have to worry about that. Trust me."

"Okay, now scat before those guys come back."

"Thanks," she said, extending her hand.

He rubbed his hands on his slacks before taking hers, turning it over and kissing the back. "My pleasure."

Luce smiled and pulled the hood over the ball cap for extra cover.

"I'll see ya later," she said, knowing it probably wouldn't happen.

"Sure." He waved her off as he turned his back and crawled into his little piece of real estate.

Steadying herself on the wall, Luce hobbled down toward the docks. Hugging the wall, she staggered. The pain in her foot was shooting up her leg with each step. Finally, she relented and ducked into an empty doorway, pushing herself up against the glass door. Plopping down, she pulled her legs up, hugging them. The hard edges of the gun cut into her stomach.

One bullet.

The cylinder spun, he laughed manically, pressed the cold steel against her head, and pulled the trigger.

Bam.

A car backfiring in the distance jolted Luce awake. She tried to focus in the pitch-black of the night. The docks weren't exactly famous for their mood lighting, so it took Luce a minute to orient herself. She hadn't slept in days. Petrov kept the hours of the dead, walking in at all times of the night, jerking her chain. When he hadn't been screwing with her, his men took pleasure in toying with her when they brought her meals or when they unchained her to pee in the bucket.

She scrubbed her face, forcing herself to wake up. The stench of rotting fish and garbage drifted in with the cold fingers of fog that cloaked her location. It was hit or miss. Cold from the fog but safe from prying eyes. It was time to find someplace warm and a phone. On cue, her stomach grumbled. Food had been sent in sparingly. Luce was sure it was used as a reward. Tell Petrov where his wife was, and she could eat. Otherwise she got what was left after everyone else ate. Petrov underestimated Luce's determination. It would be the last time he did that.

Standing, Luce pushed the shards of pain from her mind and concentrated on Brooke. She needed Luce, and Luce, well, Luce needed to get back to her lover and protect her from Petrov. If he got his hands on Brooke, he would do whatever it took to get his wife and daughter back.

The question was, would he go so far as to create a fake sister for Luce?

Probably.

Poking her head out of the doorway, Luce searched the dark street for movement. Nothing stirred at this time of night at the docks. Fishing season was over, and the warehouses wouldn't open for a while, but the dockworkers were early risers, so Luce had to get a move on if she was going to make it home. Luce would use her vagrant look to her advantage. Spotting an abandoned shopping cart, she hobbled over to it. It was full of garbage, and she pushed it slowly down the empty street. The wheels creaked, sending out a locator beacon if anyone was looking.

Headlights shone down at the end of the street.

Her heart raced. She stopped and crouched behind the cart, as if it would offer her some sort of protective cover. Her hands still on the handle, she eased her head around and watched it make a left down a side street.

She had to be quick and get off the street. A lone streetlight to her left was her destination. Luce searched the street for a pay phone. "Where's a damn phone when you need one?" she mumbled as she pushed the wobbling cart. It didn't matter. She could remember only a few numbers as it was, and she was sure everyone at the office was gone for the night. Determined, she guided the wobbling cart of garbage toward the light, resting her weight on the handle while she pushed with one foot. She smiled, remembering how, the few times when she went grocery shopping with her grandfather, he'd let her hang on the bar and he'd push her through the store. Funny how something could pop into your head when you were at your worst. Anger was also a great motivator she thought as she finally reached the corner with the streetlight.

Buildings lined the streets in all four directions. If she was looking for a landmark to guide her, she'd have better luck looking up to the skies for guidance. Warehouses meant workers, and fish processors handled their business in these warehouses. That meant there were phones in them. At least her warehouses still had landlines. So, she was hopeful technology hadn't seeped into the old buildings, yet. She'd have to commit a felony, but right now she wasn't against a little B&E, breaking and entering, to get the hell out of here. In fact, the police would be a better option than waiting for Petrov to find her. Peering into each window as she pushed her crutch down the sidewalk, she didn't see anything that stood out. She was at the end of the docks before she saw it.

A phone.

The office still had a light on in it, but nothing moved. It was almost comical the way the phone looked like it had a spotlight right on it. She waited a few minutes before she leaned against the door and gently shoved her elbow through the small pane of glass. It was too late to look for the security ribbon that lined the windows of most of the buildings on the street. Still, she waited for the sound of an alarm, her elbow wedged into the window. She was stuck.

Shit.

She tried to pull her arm free, but the shards of glass bit into Tank's thick jacket.

"Fuck me." She panicked. She needed to get free quick. She was a sitting duck for anyone who just happened by. Remembering the gun in her waistband, she pulled it and hit the glass. The sound of the shards hitting the floor echoed throughout the building.

"Great. If that doesn't bring all the boys to the yard, nothing will."

She waited for someone to pounce on her, but again, nothing moved.

Nothing.

Stepping back, she looked for a security guard that might be roaming, or running toward her because of a silent alarm.

Still nothing.

Luce walked to the door, abandoning her cart and its treasures a few yards down. Looking back into the building, she reached through and unlocked the door.

She waited.

Gently, she pushed the door a few inches.

No alarm.

Another few inches.

Still nothing.

Poking her head around the door, she searched for signs of life.

Nothing.

A conveyor and stainless-steel bins for fish. The smell was undeniable. A fish-packaging plant, closed for the season. Sardines were out of season here, but the building reeked of fish. With nothing to steal, the plant wasn't wired. God, was she about to catch a break or what?

Luce spilled around the door and silently slipped it closed. She leaned against it, gathering her strength. The adrenaline rush was seeping away, depleting any hopes she had of fighting off a potential kidnapper or security guard.

A picture of Petrov's smirk flashed in her mind. She was hell-bent on killing him. Even more now that she'd had to go through all of this. "I'm going to kill that bastard." She crawled along the wall and hid behind some crates and waited.

Nothing moved.

She edged her way to the office. Her foot throbbed with each movement, and it took everything Luce could muster not to stop and wallow in her pain. After grasping the door handle, she tried it.

Locked.

"Are you serious?" Nothing was going in her favor tonight except Tank's kindness. "So this is my best, one hundred percent." She shook her head. When a day went south, she always reminded herself that it was the best she was going to get for the day, referencing it as her 100 percent.

Luce kneeled and looked in through the window. Again, the desk lamp was spotlighting the phone, an old rotary-dial antique, tormenting her as it sat on the desk. It was telling her to come and get it, if she could. She sat back down against the door and caught her breath, momentarily letting the taunting telephone win. No sleep, no food, and the adrenaline she'd been living on for the past three days had all drained her. To top it all off, her foot was being squeezed like a vise in her boot.

"In for a penny, in for a nickel," Luce said, accounting for the deflation in the economy lately. She raised the gun to break the glass but hesitated when she spotted a pay phone across the open bay, the sign above it telling employees to limit calls to ten minutes. Then she spotted the cut line between the receiver and the phone.

"Fuck me."

She cocked back the butt of the gun, covered her face, and hit the big window in the door. This time the crash reverberated through the warehouse. Glass covered her and the floor, and she was sure it was only a matter of time now before someone came to investigate. As she pulled herself up by the handle, it sounded like she was walking on hundreds of eggshells as she crunched on the shards of glass. Grabbing the phone, she sighed when she heard the dial tone.

Thank God. Finally something was going in her favor. After she dialed her only hope, and the one number she knew by heart, it seemed to take forever, and her pulse ticked up with each ring.

"Hello, Potter home. Brooke is no able to come to phone. But maybe you can leave message with me,

Luce." Petrov's voice taunted her through the receiver.

She froze. Ice ran through her veins as rage started to boil in her gut. He was at Brooke's apartment. Where the fuck was Brooke? Sammy? Anyone?

Chapter Twenty-two

Brooke tucked her purse under her arm after extracting her car keys. Slipping out of the house wasn't the problem. Doing it without anyone noticing was. She was just about to grab the handle when the door flew open, and Sammy strode through like a man on fire.

"Oh, my apologies, Ms. Erickson." Sammy bowed.

"Sammy."

He looked her up and down, especially at her purse. Pointing at it and then the keys, he asked, "Where are you going?"

Brooke looked at the door, then down at the keys. "Out?"

"I don't think so. Boss would have my head if you went out."

"I need to find some answers, Sammy."

"Who are you expecting to tell you what's going on, Ms. Erickson?"

"I was going to visit Auntie. Maybe she can read the tattoo and tell us what it means. Maybe there's a clue in it that could help us find Luce."

Sammy held up a flash drive and waved it. "I have a clue right here, Ms. Erickson."

"What is that?"

"Video footage of the oyabun being abducted."

"What?" Brooke moved closer and whispered,

"We need to call Colby."

"Not yet." Sammy locked the front door and walked past Brooke. "I'm not sure you should see this, Ms. Erickson."

"The hell you say," Brooke said, following close behind Sammy.

Sammy met Sasha in the hallway, whispered something, and motioned toward the study. They were on a mission to get their boss back, and Brooke admired them for it. Sammy stuck the drive into the computer, wiggled the mouse, and waited for the screen to activate. Clicking on a file, Sammy sat back and watched the drama unfold before him.

Brooke watched. Even though she anticipated something was going to happen, she gasped as she saw someone toss something over Luce's head, punch her in the stomach, and shove her into another SUV parked next to hers.

"Play it again?"

"Ms. Erickson—"

"Play it again," she demanded.

Doing as he was told, Sammy hit the Play button on the video player.

"Enlarge it."

Sammy clicked the upper right-hand corner and filled the screen with the video.

Everyone watched as Luce pulled up to the flower shop and got out of her car. Then she pointed her fob at the car just as another car took the empty space next to her. Two men jumped out of the SUV next to hers, tossed something over her head, and pummeled her before tossing her in the backseat of the SUV.

Brooke covered her mouth. "Play it again."

The video played out again, and this time Sammy

and Sasha crowded the screen looking closer at the SUV.

"Stop," Sasha said, pointing to the license plate. "Can you make that out?"

Sammy backed the video up to the point where the SUV pulled next to Luce's car. The letters and numbers were difficult to see.

"It looks like S…3…8…I can't make out the rest," Sasha said, shaking her head.

"We need to give this to Agent Water. She'll have the resources to clean up the footage."

Sammy looked at Sasha and then at Brooke. Pulling a copy of the video to the computer desktop, he ejected the flash drive and handed it to Brooke.

"It's your call, Ms. Erickson." He offered a weak smile before returning his attention to the video file.

Brooke watched as they played it over and over again. She needed to get that flash drive into the hands of Colby. She'd be able to clean up the video, run the plates, and find out who owned the SUV, but she suspected she already knew who the owner was. Petrov.

༄༄༄༄

Colby stood behind the group craning their necks to get a better view of the video they'd already viewed thousands of times.

"Where did you get this?"

No one answered.

"I'm asking you a question. Where did you get this?" Colby's tone was menacing.

"Isn't it obvious, Agent Water?" Sammy said, not bothering to look at her.

"Okay, let me rephrase that—how did you get

this?"

Colby looked at the two in front of her, then at Brooke.

"I have no idea."

"Really?"

Brooke shrugged and turned back to the screen. "Do you think you can find enough on this to help find Luce?"

"It looks promising. I'm just pissed no one gave us this information when we asked."

"You're getting it now, Agent Water," Sammy said. "You just have to know how to grease the wheels."

"You mean rough up the witnesses?"

"We didn't use violence to get this information. These shop owners are just more likely to want to help the oyabun than the police."

Brooke pulled Colby aside. Watching the verbal sparring match just to see whose dick was bigger was pissing her off, and it was doing nothing to find Luce.

"Look, you have new evidence that could help find Luce. Can you just run with it?"

"You mean look the other way?"

"I don't care what you call it. Find Luce. You've been given a freebie, and you didn't have to compromise yourself or your job. Please, find Luce."

Colby tossed the jump drive into the air and caught it a few times before she finally responded. "Fine. I'll let you know what I find out."

"Thank you."

Colby slammed the door as she left the study, making everyone jump.

"Okay, so what's the plan?" Brooke pushed her head between the two still staring at the monitor.

Sammy sat back and turned, looking at Brooke.

"We don't have a plan. I have a lead on Frank. As for Petrov, we're working on it."

"Petrov is the one who has Luce. That's obvious, since the guys who nabbed her were Caucasian."

"True, but the oyabun wanted me to find Frank, and I have."

"So what now?" Sasha asked.

"Frank is Mei's father," Brooke blurted out.

Both looked at Brooke, clearly surprised.

"You're shitting me," Sasha said. "My apologies, Ms. Erickson."

"No worries. We were just as surprised as you two are. Near as I can figure, Frank took Mei away from her birth mother and raised her with another woman. If I were guessing, I'd say Mei is JP's daughter. Maybe he had an affair with a woman, maybe he was married to her, but I'm starting to think JP never knew he had another daughter."

"But why would Frank do all of that and not tell JP?"

Brooke shrugged and shook her head. "Blackmail."

"Blackmail?" both asked in unison.

"Luce's grandfather would have wanted to protect Luce's sister, even if JP was the father. Family meant everything to him, and Luce having a sister, well..." Brooke looked at Sammy and then Sasha, who were both nodding in agreement. She didn't need to say the rest. Family was job number one. Whether you picked them or they were blood kin, you protected your family no matter what. "So, find Frank. Watch for the right time and nab him. No eyes, no witnesses, and no loose ends. Luce will want him here when she gets back."

"But what about Petrov?"

"He better hope Colby gets him first. 'Cause if Luce does, he's a dead man."

"And what are we supposed to do with Mrs. Petrov and Kat?"

Brooke thought for a moment. They needed to tighten things up, quick. "Have someone bring them back and put them in the apartment at the club. They'll be easier to control and guard. We're too spread out, and we need to have everyone home."

"You're starting to sound like the oyabun," Sammy said, then smiled.

"Definitely," Sasha said, standing and grabbing her gun she'd laid on the desk and tucking it into the holster against her rib. "I'll tell Momo to get the girls."

"Did you pick up those supplies I asked for, Sasha?"

"I did. They're in Luce's office."

"Thanks."

"For you?"

"No." Brooke patted Sasha on the shoulder. "Sammy, when can you get Frank?"

"He thinks he's pretty well hidden, so I can probably get him soon."

"Do it. I want you to take him to the warehouse. Lock him in a cage, gag him, do whatever it takes to shut him up. If he fights you, do what it takes to make him understand that his days are numbered."

She noticed Sammy's stunned look as she barked out orders. Her back was against the wall, and she wasn't about to let everything fall apart because her lover wasn't here. Luce needed someone to find her, capture Frank, and bring Petrov to bear for his decision to abduct her.

Oh, he was going to pay all right.

"Let me know when the women are in the city, Sasha. You get Frank and I'll watch Mei. We don't need any slip-ups. Understood?" Brooke absentmindedly pointed at each member of Luce's crew.

"No fuck-ups."

"Yes, Ms. Erickson." Both bowed.

"What about Mei?" Sasha asked.

"I'll take care of her."

Sasha's confused look made Brooke laugh. "I do have a gun, and I know how to use it. Besides, thanks to Sammy, we have a great security system."

"But—"

"I know how to dial 9-1-1."

"Yes, ma'am."

"Go. Call me after you both finish."

"Yes, ma'am." Both bowed and backed out of the room.

If they didn't like taking orders from Brooke, that was too bad. She was going to make sure Luce's absence didn't mean that everything had to grind to a stop. Brooke wavered with a rush of adrenaline. *So, this is what it's like to have power and make people follow your every word without argument. Wow.*

Now she needed to see one more person, and then she could relax.

༄༅༄༅

Brooke gently tapped on the door of the guest room Mei was staying in.

"Mei?"

"Yes, Ms. Erickson?" Mei opened the door and peeked out, looking around Brooke.

"I brought you something." Brook held up a bag.

"Oh." Mei's eyes lit up. She opened the door wider and ushered Brooke in. Closing it gently behind her, she said, "Where is Sasha?"

"She's a little busy."

"Okay," she said, excitement lacing her voice.

"May I?" Brooke pointed to the bed. It looked like it hadn't been slept in, with its tight corners and smooth cover.

"Please." Mei kept her eyes on the white bag Brooke was holding. Sitting next to Brooke, she vibrated with energy, patting her knees and fidgeting.

"I thought you might like to have something to do while we try to figure out what's going on." Brooke placed the bag, one side down, on Mei's lap.

"Oh, that is very nice of you to think of my comfort." Mei placed her hand on the bag, waiting.

"Open it, please."

After pulling the handle apart, Mei peeked inside the bag. Her eyes widened, and her face split with a giant smile. "I can't accept this gift. It's too much." Mei closed her eyes and shut the bag.

"Nonsense. I would be honored to see your work. Besides…" Brooke took Mei's hand and smiled. "I'm sure Luce would, too."

Mei smiled and peered into the bag again then wiggled her shoulders. Reaching inside she pulled out each item and laid watercolors, brushes, paper, pencils, pens, and ink and meticulously placed them on the duvet.

"Words are…words cannot express my gratitude, Ms. Erickson."

"Mei, please call me Brooke."

"Yes, Miss Brooke." Mei looked like as if she was

afraid to touch the art supplies. Finally she picked up a brush and ran her finger over the bristles.

"Are they good enough?"

"Oh yes, they are wonderful, Miss Brooke." Mei laid the brush back on the bed and touched each item, almost as if handling them would make them disappear.

"Well, I'll leave you to them. Please let me know if you need anything."

"Oh, Miss Brooke, may I give you a hug?" Mei's face colored with embarrassment.

"Of course."

It was quick and distant, but it was a hug nonetheless. Baby steps, Brooke told herself. Baby steps.

"Would you like me to have a snack sent up? Maybe to tide you over until we eat?"

"No, I'm sorry. I'm too excited to eat. My apologies."

"Don't apologize. I'll check in on you later."

"Yes." Mei opened the watercolor box. "Thank you again, Miss Brooke."

"My pleasure."

Brooke gently closed the door and leaned on it. One problem down, two more to solve. It was going to be a long night.

Brooke pulled out her phone and tapped the face. "Do you have an update yet?"

Chapter Twenty-three

"Luce? Is this you? Of course it's you. How the fuck are you?" Petrov laughed.

There was no way Sammy would let him get to Brooke. No way. Luce's breathing was so erratic she had to cover the receiver. She shook with rage. All she could think about was killing that bastard, a slow, painful death, and she'd take great pleasure in making it last for days.

"Luce? he asked, laughing. "Oh, Luce…"

She didn't respond. Without waiting, she slammed the receiver down. Sammy would never be there with Petrov. He'd take every precaution to protect Brooke. His life depended on it. Dialing another number, she called her home, let it ring twice, and then hung up. It had been her signal years ago, when she was younger and didn't want her grandfather to answer the phone. She'd wait a minute and dial again. God, she hoped the staff remembered the signal.

Running her fingers in continuous circles around the face of the dial, she sat waiting for someone to pick up. She tapped the desk nervously.

Nothing.

Shit.

By her own design, everyone was on lockdown, which meant no one would answer the phones after hours, especially from numbers they didn't recognize. Great. She was the victim of her own efficiency.

"Fuck," she screamed at the top of her lungs. She didn't care who found her now. The police were more than welcome at this point. At least she'd get to the hospital and have her foot checked out, three squares and a cot, and a phone call to her lawyer.

Maggie.

The Dungeon would still be open, and Maggie would be prowling the halls looking for her next bondage beefcake. Luce doubted Petrov knew anything about Luce's connection to The Dungeon. She was protective of that part of her life, and it'd been almost a year since she'd been to see Maggie on a professional level. Hell, Sammy didn't even know about Maggie, so there was no way she would be compromised. Luce stared at the phone, trying to remember The Dungeon's number, or even Gail's private number. Nothing was bubbling to the top.

Think, think, think, she chanted over and over. Come on. She pressed her fingers to her temples and rubbed. The screen of her phone flashed in her mind. Gail's picture and number popped up. At least she hoped it was her number.

Dialing it, she waited.

"Shlesinger resident. This better be good," the sleep-laden voice said on the other end.

"Sorry, wrong number." Luce slammed down the receiver. "Shit."

She had to hurry. No telling what would walk through that door, and it was getting close to the split-shifters, who usually started showing up at three a.m. for work.

Think, think.

She tried the same number but this time changed out the two for a four.

"You've reached the Ralph household. Leave a message, and someone in this nutty house will call you back. Don't be surprised if it's the squirrel," a young voice said. "How was that, Mom?" he said in the background before the beep went off.

"Damn."

She was sure it was close to that number. Changing one more digit, she ran her fingers around the rotary face, again.

"The Dungeon."

"Finally." Luce bent over and eased her elbows down on the desk, relief accelerating through her body.

A beam of light hit her. She looked up at her shadow being broadcast on the wall in front of her. "Fuck."

"Don't move."

"Excuse me. Who is this?"

Luce had just hit a crossroad, both physically and mentally. Did she put her hands up and comply, or did she get help from the person on the other end of the phone? Closing her eyes, she remembered the cold steel in her waistband, which would end this dilemma immediately. The only problem she was grappling with was that the man behind her sounded as if peach fuzz was barely an option when he'd decided to shave that day. Gail waited on the other end of this mess, while behind her stood a security guard, who, if he was carrying a gun, she hoped had a trigger finger trained for control.

"Can I speak to Gail, please. This is an emergency. Tell her Luce Potter is on the line," she said as she laid the phone down and put her hands in the air.

Chapter Twenty-four

Brooke sat in a warm bath. Tendrils of steam floated and coated the air with moisture. Screw the doctors, she thought. The bullet wound on her left side, though bright pink, looked like it was almost healed. She'd taped a plastic covering over it, just in case, but she was having a bath, damn it. Jasmine and lavender oils skated across the surface of the water. Brooke dragged her finger through the odd-shaped puddles, bisecting them and then swirling around in them.

She wondered how Luce was being treated. Her mind was filled with thoughts of her lover. Was Petrov feeding her, or was he trying to beat the location of his wife and daughter out of her? Brooke worried for her safety. Luce's pain tolerance was high. She'd seen her practically bleeding to death and still carry Brooke's own broken body to safety, without a care for her own life. Hopefully, Sammy would have news of Luce's location, and they could figure out how to get to her. As for the women, Brooke didn't intend to take any chances. They would be her chit to get Luce out of Petrov's clutches.

Now Frank, he was another story. They had to make sure he was alive and breathing when they got Luce back. She'd want to handle him personally. The issue of Mei made it a sticky situation and one she would gladly let Luce handle. There were no winners in that situation. Luce wanted Frank dead, and Mei had no idea Frank probably wasn't her father, but she loved him like a father. Perhaps they could find a way to expose Frank's treachery and still save Mei from the loss of him. On the other hand, they could just kill him and never tell Mei the truth.

Suddenly, Brooke had a thought. If Mei's recollection was right, Frank had basically bought her from her real family. Perhaps Brooke could find them and reunite Mei with her birth mother. It could lessen the devastating news that Frank had ripped a baby from its mother's arms and hopefully turn Mei against him. It was risky, but it was a plan.

She'd have to think about it further. Right now, she needed to wait for everything to come together so she could put a team out there to find her lover. Luce was her main priority. She needed her home, in her bed, and safe, period.

Sliding down farther into the tub, she let the scented hot water work its healing magic on her soul. She worked on clearing her head, focused on each breath she took in and out, in and out. She wasn't good at meditation, but she's seen her lover do it enough times and centered herself. Her mind eased into a relaxed state as she thought of nothing.

Emptiness.

Luce's face slipped in and she smiled at the memory. It was the first time they'd met. Luce had had a certain sex appeal, wearing her leathers and straddling her "iron horse," as she called it.

Out of the corner of her eye, a flash in the rearview mirror caught her attention. A motorcycle streaked within inches of her door. The driver hugged the metal monster, now sliding sideways in front of her car. Brooke slammed on her brakes and gasped when the back wheel of the bike bucked into the air, like a horse trying to dislodge its rider. Miraculously, the driver rode the front tire a few more feet and dropped the back tire solidly onto the ground. She was amazed when the bike finally stopped in the middle of the road. Brooke's car jerked to a stop only a few feet from where the driver straddled the raging machine. The engine issued a throaty protest as its rider gunned the throttle, then turned it off.

Brooke sat stunned as the long body of the driver unfolded off the bike and dropped the kickstand. The tall, sinewy figure looked as though it had been dipped in black leather, the bodysuit conforming to every ridge and muscle on the rider's body. When the rider turned, Brooke got her first view of a very feminine form stomping toward her. She cringed as the woman punched her hand into her palm with each step, moving closer.

Luce controlled the motorcycle as she controlled her life. Strong and in charge. Her body molded to the machine as if it were just an extension of herself. She had ridden with Luce a few times, but she had to be honest. It just wasn't her thing. The thought of purposely taking your life in your hands, watching the asphalt pass under your feet and the curves under your knees, practically made Brooke eat her heart once or twice when it ended up in her throat. No, that was one pleasure she was willing to relinquish to her lover. However, any chance she had to see Luce in the leathers or take her out of them was reward enough.

She let her head rest on the side of the tub and felt herself drifting off.

Brooke had heard the motorcycle eating up the gravel as it made its way onto the property. Running down the hall, through the walkway to the garage, she caught sight of Luce maneuvering the throaty, rumbling machine to a stop. She kicked down the stand and peeled her helmet off.

"Wanna help me?" Luce smiled, tossing the helmet onto the workbench in the garage.

"Hey, sexy," Brooke said, sauntering over to Luce, who was still straddling the metal monster.

"Hey, beautiful. Wanna go for a little ride around the property?"

"Uh-uh." She moved close enough that Luce pulled her hips against her, keeping her from touching the still-hot machine and running her gloved hands down the curve of Brooke's hip.

"So, what did you have in mind?" Luce quirked an eyebrow and then offered Brooke a salacious grin. "Or maybe I can guess."

Brooke's practical lack of clothing left little to the imagination. Shorts and a tank top made for easy access for what Brooke had in mind. All she needed was a willing participant, and she knew her lover too well not to have come prepared.

Running her hands over Luce's leather-covered chest, she seductively flicked her tongue over her lips, wetting them, and then looked up at Luce.

"Oh, so you want to play like that, do you?"

"Do I?" Brooke let her hands roam the tight, lean frame of her lover. She slid her hand up into Luce's hair, releasing the ponytail she kept it in when riding. Fanning out the smooth hair, she glided her hand up farther into Luce's scalp and gently held Luce. Her lips attacked Luce's with a ferocity that surprised her lover, if her gasp was any indication.

Brooke found the zipper to the front of Luce's leathers, and, pulling it, she exposed the sports bra underneath. Tugging on the shoulders of the tight leather, she released Luce's arms but pushed them behind her back.

"Why, my love, what do you have in mind?" Luce teased.

Brooke bent down and bit Luce's breast through her bra. The nipple hardened instantly. Moving to the other side, she repeated the action, only this time she tweaked the nipple she'd just excited. Luce's hands threaded into her hair, and she held Brooke tight against her breast.

Slipping the zipper down farther, Brooke went down on her knees and mouthed Luce's mound. A rasped cry escaped Luce's lips. Brooke smiled. Pushing the panties to the side, she let her tongue spear at what she wanted. Moving in closer, Brooke's tongue spread the cleft of Luce's lips and lavished her tongue on the hard clit.

"Surely you want to take this to our room?" Luce grunted out.

"Hmm, no." Brooke pulled on Luce's panties and stopped. The leathers were in the way. "Damn."

"Maybe I can be of assistance," Luce offered, frantically straining to get her leathers down to her knees.

"Thank you."

Brooke pressed Luce's hips against the motorcycle and pressed her knees apart just enough to get access and buried her head between Luce's legs.

Brooke could feel Luce thread her fingers in her

hair and gently hold her. Running her hands up Luce's body, she yanked the sports bra up and palmed Luce's breasts. Working her clit at the same time. Luce had always told her that riding her motorcycle was akin to riding a giant vibrator, the pounding orgasm a testament to how quickly she was coming right now.

"Christ," Luce moaned. Her body wound tight as Brooke pushed her harder. Luce heaved and jerked Brooke to her feet as she spasmed again. "Stop. I don't think I can handle another one."

Their lips intertwined, Luce demanded entrance, and Brooke obliged, feeling Luce's tongue practically devouring her.

"Sure you don't want to take that ride? I can promise it will be worth it," Luce said, whispering in Brooke's ear.

That was how their love life was—passionate, consuming, and sexy.

"I'm good." Brooke smiled. "But I can go for another taste, if you're willing."

"Babe, if I do that again, I won't be able to stand. How about you and I..." Luce nodded toward the door.

The garage door cranked down as Brooke tried to pull Luce's leathers to her hips.

"You're just so sexy in that leather, honey. I couldn't help myself."

"What if someone saw us?" Luce cradled Brooke's body against hers.

"Now you're shy?"

"Well..."

Brooke leaned against Luce's taut body and ran her hands down her rib cage, softly scratching a path to Luce's center.

"I didn't say that, but there are eyes around here,

you know."

"*Only mine, and what I'm looking at is...*" Brooke tweaked a nipple. "*Is mine.*"

"How about we discuss this in a hot bath and a glass of wine?"

"*I don't think we can swim in wine, lover,*" Brooke joked.

"You know what I mean." Luce swatted Brooke's ass as she walked away, pulling Luce behind her.

"Later."

"Ms. Erickson?" Celeste said on the other side of the bathroom door. "Mr. Sammy is back."

Brooke instinctively covered herself as she woke from the daydream. "I'll be right out."

"Yes, Ms. Erickson."

Brooke eased out of the bath and hurried to dry herself. Hopefully, Sammy had news for her about Luce. Slipping into sweatpants, she poked at her wound, still bright pink. After covering it with a fresh bandage, she slid a sweatshirt on. God, how she suddenly loved flexible clothing. She gently rubbed the side of her face. She must have been gritting her teeth, because her jaw ached. Luckily, it wasn't broken, but a few teeth on that side of her face had been fractured when Frank had slammed his meaty fist into her face. He'd pay for that and so much more, when she got him.

Walking into the study, Sammy stood at attention, waiting for Brooke to say something.

"What's the news, Sammy?"

Chapter Twenty-five

"Please don't shoot." Thinking quick, Luce added, "I just wanted to get warm."

"You damn homeless people. Christ."

Luce heard footfalls coming closer, and then she heard Maggie pick up the phone.

"Luce, Luce, where the hell are you? My phone has been ringing off the hook. Brooke is sick with worry."

"Officer, please don't shoot me," Luce yelled, hoping Maggie could hear her.

"Oh, shit." Maggie had heard her.

"I thought this was an abandoned warehouse. Please don't shoot."

"Oh, Jesus, Luce," Maggie whispered. "Which warehouse?"

"Get down on your knees."

"Come on, Officer. Who comes down here to the fishing docks on the weekend? I'll be gone in the morning. Have some pity on an old homeless woman."

"You broke the windows. Someone's gonna have to pay for those." He hesitated, edging closer to Luce.

"I'll pay for the damages. What's the owner's name of this building on the waterfront?"

Luce was hoping Maggie was paying attention. She was all but drawing her a picture of her location.

"Doesn't matter. You're gonna go to jail and get a hot meal and a shower. God knows you need it if that stench is coming from you."

"Sit tight, Luce. I'm on my way. I'll call Sammy."

"No, not Sammy," Luce blurted out.

"Who the heck is Sammy? Oh, great. You're one of those wacko street people."

"Gotcha. I'm on my way," Maggie said, hanging up.

The drone of the dead line, the only lifeline Luce had to her life, echoed from the table.

"Hey, who you trying to call?"

The security guard instinctively reached for the phone, listened, and then hung up the receiver.

Luce looked up at the kid. Peach fuzz splotched his chin, and a poor attempt at a mustache barely lined his upper lip.

"Jesus, what happened to you?" His gaze darted from her bruised and swollen eyes to her bloodied nose and then her split lip. "No wonder you're hiding."

He knelt down and studied her face, a compassionate expression replacing the forced stern look he'd presented earlier. Luce felt bad for the kid. He wasn't cut out for this kinda work. Eventually someone would chew him up and spit what was left to the ground, a broken spirit who'd chosen the wrong profession. Well, that wasn't her problem. She needed to get out of here before the audience grew bigger.

He reached for something behind his back, and Luce pushed back away from him. Throwing up his right hand, he presented his left, holding a water bottle.

"Whoa, just relax. You must be thirsty." He shoved it toward Luce. "What's your name?"

Luce locked eyes with the man whose nametag said—just as generic as his blond hair, blue-eyed look did—Smith.

"What's your name? Who did this to you?"

Luce shook her head and scooted away from him. Playing her part to the max, she dropped her eyes and scrunched the water bottle nervously.

"Maeve." Sounded older, she thought. Her eyes were so swollen he wouldn't be able to guess her ethnicity. So she kept it simple. "You gonna call the cops?"

Smith shook his head. He squatted eye level with Luce and stared at the marks on her face. He was making her squirm with the scrutiny, and she was suddenly uncomfortable.

"I should, but..."

"I'll leave. I just...well, I was just runnin' and...well, this looked like a safe place to hide."

She lowered her face submissively. "I got some cash here somewhere." She made a show of patting her oversized pants. She was stalling in hopes Maggie would get here soon. The gun in her pants was her last alternative. She didn't want to hurt the kid, but she'd do whatever it took to keep her own life. "I don't put it in my pockets, 'cause that's the first place them gangbangers look, so I keep it..." Luce reached down the front of her pants, the huge jacket covering her revolver.

"It's fine. Look, I can see someone has rumbled all over your face, and God only knows what the rest of you looks like, So, no fast moves, but don't you stand up, and I'll get you some coffee and clean up this mess. The guy who owns this warehouse isn't the nicest guy. I'm going to have to let him know what happened here."

He reached down and grabbed Luce's arm, pulling her up, while her hand was around the gun in her waistband. "Mr. Petrov is kinda a bastard."

Luce froze. Petrov owned the warehouse. How ironic.

"Okay." Luce stood and rested her hands on the desk. If the kid felt the need to alert Petrov, he would know it was her. So she'd have no choice but to kill the kid. Luce groaned and doubled over.

"Are you okay," he said, bending with her.

"I don't feel so well."

"Here, let me help—"

Luce jerked up and pulled the gun from her waistband, pushing the security guard backward on his back and straddling him. She had the muzzle under his nose.

Wide-eyed, Smith squeaked out, "Don't kill me." His hands were up, cupping his ears, as if that would protect his head.

"No offense, kid, but I can't let you make that call."

"What?"

"Put your hands out above your head and flip over," she ordered him.

He struggled underneath her weight for a moment, but the click of the hammer hastened his speed, and he was finally able to lie flat on his stomach.

"You want to live to see tomorrow, stay on your stomach."

He made a show of pushing his hands out as far as he could and then froze.

Luce pushed the muzzle to the base of his skull. "Cuffs?"

He shook his head. Aw, he was a rent-a-cop. Luce shook her own head. The badge stitched onto his jacket was just for show, a low-level intimidation tactic. She looked down at his waist and saw a plain duty belt with mace, a few zip-ties, and a walkie-talkie. Brilliant.

"I'm going to take off your belt. Don't even flinch." She pushed the muzzle harder into his neck.

Sliding her hand under his belly, she yanked his duty belt off. "You're right, your boss is a bastard."

He lay silent.

"Take your clothes off."

"What?"

"Take your clothes off. Sorry, kid, but I'm thinking you won't be chasing me down the street naked. So strip."

When he didn't move, her hands pushed under his belly again, she undid the button on his pants. Little twerp. He raised his hips, and she could feel his hard-on. Christ. She stood and pulled his pants along with his boxers off. His hips flinched when he hit the cold, hard floor.

"Serves you right. Who the fuck gets a hard-on when they might be shot," she said. "Who?"

"Sorry."

Luce pulled his boots and socks off with one hand, while her gun created a permanent indentation at the base of his skull.

"Don't even think about trying anything. You have no idea who you're dealing with, and I don't want your death on my conscience." She pushed the boots and socks to the side. "Sorry, kid. This isn't personal. Let me give you a little advice. Quit your job. Petrov finds out you let me live, and you'll be dead before you can finish telling him the story."

"But—"

"I'm Luce Potter." She looked down at him and made eye contact.

He mouthed an "Oh."

"I'm doing you a favor right now." Without a second thought, Luce raised the butt of the gun and clocked him on the side of the head. Out cold.

"Trust me. This will work out better for you this way. At least he'll think I jumped you."

Luce rolled the kid over and took his jacket. The spring of his dick almost made her laugh. Oh, to be young, dumb, and full of…She pushed back on his sprung member and pulled his elbows together, zip-tied them, and then tied his wrists. She put him on his side and grabbed his ankles and tied them, too. He wasn't going anywhere fast.

Grabbing his clothes she set them on the desk and picked up the phone and dialed Maggie, again.

"Luce? What the fuck is going on?"

"Oh, thank God you haven't left yet." Luce realized it would have been a huge mistake to have Maggie patrolling the docks looking for her. Now she could work out a plan that just might keep them both out of danger. "Maggie, I need you to listen carefully."

Luce gave her detailed instructions. She was to tell no one, not even Sammy or Brooke, that she was alive. She was to get in her car and drive out of town on the old service road that would take her past the airport, then double back and head down to the warehouse district, find the only liquor store, get there in exactly forty minutes, and wait for her. If she didn't show up in two minutes, she was to leave.

"Two minutes, Luce. That's not enough time to stop the car, turn off the engine, and wait."

"If I'm there, it'll be more than enough time. If I'm not, it'll be barely enough time to get yourself out of there before someone tries to arrest you for prostitution, or from being approached by a pro."

Luce had noticed several working girls walking around the only light in the district. Like moths to a flame, they congregated where they could be checked out, bargained for, and pick up their trick. These weren't your garden-variety working girls either. These were Petrov's girls, working off a debt. He was the biggest white slaver on the West Coast, and they didn't hang around long. As soon as they were worn out, he disposed of them in inhumane ways. At least that's what she'd heard. Dead women don't tell tales if they aren't breathing and can't be found.

"If I'm not there, drive off. I'll find another way to get to The Dungeon. Right now it's the safest place. Petrov doesn't know you, and I want to keep it that way."

"But Luce—"

"Maggie. Don't talk to anyone. Period." Her voice was stern.

"But what about Brooke?"

"I'll explain everything later. Remember, if I'm not there, leave. Do.Not.Get.Out.Of.Your.Car. Do you understand me?"

"Okay."

"Thanks, Maggie."

"Of course."

"And Maggie, bring a gun."

"Luce, you're scaring me."

Smith started to stir.

"I've got to go, Maggie. Do exactly as I said. Don't drive directly here. Understand?"

"I got it. I got it."

Luce put the receiver in the cradle and stared at it for a moment. This had to work, or she feared she wouldn't get the hell out of there alive. Luce yanked the line from the phone to the wall and grabbed Smith's boxers. Shoving them into his mouth, she wrapped the line around his head.

"This is for your own good," she whispered in his ear. "When you talk to Petrov, tell him Luce Potter is coming for him." She whacked him on the back of the head again, expanding the red welt even more. "Sorry."

The black uniform helped conceal Luce. Tucking her long black hair up under the ball cap with the security logo on it took a good ten minutes. Each time she pushed, a strand fell out on the other side. Finally, she just bent over, twisted it all together, fed it into the ball cap, and pushed it onto her head. She had to do that a couple of times. Seemed Smith had a big head, and Luce couldn't get the snaps on the back quite right. She laughed to herself. If this was the worst thing to happen to her tonight, her life was changing course. She slipped the oversize jacket on over the jacket she had from Bob.

Riffling through the pockets, she found a pack of Spearmint gum, the kind that came in a five-stick pack. She lifted it to her nose and took a long sniff. She would eat the whole pack if it could keep her hunger at bay. Slipping it back into the pocket, she looked in the other. Mostly trash, receipts for pizza and soda, a condom—no surprise there—and his ID tag. She clipped the badge to the collar of the jacket and stood up straight. Funny how wearing a uniform did that to people, she thought. Pulling the belt tighter around her slim waist, she tossed Smith's boots into the trash bin and walked toward the door. Well, she limped toward the door. If she wasn't careful, that would be the one thing that would give her away tonight.

Gently pulling the door behind her, she peeked out and looked down the street, first to the right and then to the left. The cold, wet fog slapped her in the face, a reminder that she shouldn't be venturing out this late. Pulling her collar tight around her neck, she took out the key ring she'd swiped from Smith and swung the keys like she was bored. She looked into a building, flashing the stream of light up and down the floor as if she were Smith. When she didn't see anyone, she tried to bob and weave through the dark streets. Ducking into a doorway, she popped her head out long enough to see if anyone was walking in her direction. She slid against the wall, then ducked into another and then another. She was forty minutes and blocks away from the liquor store she'd spotted earlier. It was proving to be the longest forty minutes of her life.

"Hey, Smith? Coffee at three?"

Luce froze. How far away was the man who'd just called out to her, to Smith? Pulling the collar up she turned and checked him out. He was far enough that he couldn't make her out, so she waved and replied in a gruff voice. "Three."

"Your turn to buy."

"Yep."

She kept walking, his footsteps going in the opposite direction. Luce darted into a darkened alcove and bent over, leaning on her knees, ready to hurl. Some badass Yakuza she was. A guy calls out for coffee, and she's ready to keel over from a heart attack.

"Buck up, sister," she told herself. "You've been in worse scrapes than this. Christ."

Looking down at the oversize watch she'd snatched, she felt bad now that she'd taken practically everything Smith had on him. Maggie was probably still a good twenty minutes away from the liquor store. Smith was known down on the docks. She couldn't just stop doing rounds. The other guys would get suspicious. So Luce hustled a little quicker and made her way toward her destination.

A few women strolled in front of the liquor store, stopping and talking to each other until a car pulled up to the curb. A guy signaled one over, and she ducked her head into the open window, just like Mrs. Petrov had when Luce had grabbed her in the hospital garage. The woman waved to her friend, slid daintily into the front seat, and cozied over to the man. His slithering smile made Luce want to puke. The other two women went back to chatting and walking. They looked up the street and then back down the street; their lips and hips never stopped moving.

Luce eased closer to the store but tried to keep her distance as she waited for Maggie. Looking the way she did, the prostitutes would take her for a curb crawler, and she didn't need any extra attention. At least not right now.

Maggie's black sedan rolled up to the liquor store, and right on cue the ladies of the night sauntered over to the car and tapped on the window. Luce chuckled. If they only knew what Maggie did as a sideline, they'd cut her a wide path. Hobbling over to the door, Luce looked at one of the working girls and smiled.

"Excuse me, ladies. She's waiting for me." Luce

bent down, pulled her ball cap off, and tapped the window. "Maggie?"

The locks of the sedan popped, allowing Luce to slide past the hookers and sit down.

"Jesus, Luce." Maggie locked the doors and started to pull away from the curb. "What's that smell?"

"I need a shower." Luce ducked down and rolled her seat back so she could stretch her legs. If she could amputate her foot she'd feel ten times better; the pain was starting to radiate up her leg. "Drive down to the docks and then back up one street over. I don't want any company on the way back to The Dungeon."

"Don't you want me to take you home?"

"Nope."

"Okay. What the hell happened? Sammy has stopped looking for you. He wouldn't tell me anything. Only that he was hunting you."

"Petrov, that's what happened."

"Petrov, the Russian?"

"Yep. The bastard kidnapped me." Luce closed her eyes and covered her face with the ball cap.

"What the fuck?"

"Exactly."

"Why? Where's Brooke?"

"Home, I hope."

"Oh, Christ, Luce."

The conversation was light on the way back to The Dungeon. Luce slipped in and out of sleep, each stop jarring her awake. "I'm sorry about the smell, Mag. I've been pissing in a bucket and haven't had a shower in days."

"Maybe it's better if I don't know what happened. That way, when the police contact me, I won't have to lie."

"They aren't going to contact you. I'm sure the guy I killed won't even make the news."

"Shit, Luce."

"It was me or him. I had no choice. You have to know that, Maggie."

Luce caught Maggie nodding. Thank God she'd thought of calling her. Maggie was her only phone-a-friend she could think of that wouldn't raise suspicion with Petrov.

"What did he do to you?"

"Honestly?" Luce pulled the hoodie off and sat up. She flipped the visor down and looked into the lighted mirror.

Maggie gasped as she saw Luce clearly for the first time. "What the—" Maggie pulled the car over to the side of the street and parked it. Turning, she stared at Luce's face and reached out to touch it. Luce flinched away.

"I'm fine. Just get me out of here." Luce looked around the street and sat back in the seat, hugging herself. She hated that she looked like a punching bag, but even more, she hated that Petrov had gotten the best of her, for now. He'd regret his error in judgment. She'd see to that.

"You look like shit."

"I don't want Brooke to see me like this, so take me to your place or The Dungeon. Then I need to get a message to Sammy. I don't want Brooke to worry."

"Too late. I'm sure she's frantic."

"Have you talked to her?"

"No, but I'd be freaked out if I hadn't heard from you in days." Maggie took hold of Luce's hand. Rubbing her thumb against the back of it, she said, "Luce, you have to let go of this vendetta against Petrov. I'm afraid it's going to kill you."

"It won't, but I won't rest until I have Frank, so…" She thought of all the shit she'd taken from Petrov—the deal with Deputy Chapel, the prostitution, the drugs, everything he'd done to try to ruin her reputation. She'd let him off easy before. She hadn't wanted a turf war. But now everything was fair game. She had his wife and daughter, and she'd use them to get to Frank, but now even Petrov was on the table.

Bastard.

"Do you happen to have any water or something to drink?"

Maggie reached down and pulled her coffee cup out of the holder. "Not coffee, so sip it."

"One for the road?"

"Well, after our phone call, I needed some courage."

The alcohol burned as it hit the cuts in her mouth. "Jesus, what the hell is that, moonshine?"

"Close. I told you to sip it." Maggie turned and then made another turn and focused on the street ahead. "What are you going to tell Brooke?"

"As little as possible."

"She isn't dumb, Luce. She'll know, and if you don't tell her, she'll think you're keeping something from her."

"I am."

"Don't treat her like that, Luce. She's not a child."

Luce shot Maggie a glance that said mind your own business.

"Don't even give me that look. I know what you're thinking, so stop."

Maggie was as close to a best friend as Luce had, with the exception of Brooke, and Maggie knew

Luce better than anyone, so she'd earned the right to challenge her, and she often did, at least when they'd spent more time together in the past.

"She was in the hospital because of me. I don't want her involved any more than she already is, Maggie."

The alcohol was already having an effect on Luce's equilibrium, so she put her head back on the headrest and watched the streetlights pass. What was she going to tell Brooke?

Luce punched the key fob, locking her SUV in front of the flower shop. Brooke was on her way home, and she wanted to fill the house with flowers. After the quick stop she'd made it a point to get Brooke her favorite latte at the Vanilla Bean coffee shop. It all happened so quick. Someone came up behind her, poked a gun in her ribs, put a bag over her head, and pushed her into a car parked next to her SUV. It was right out of one of those videos they showed women on how to be safe. Luce hadn't paid attention to her surroundings, too excited that Brooke was finally where she belonged. She fought back, kicking and trying to bite anything she could through the bag.

"Fucking bitch. Hit her." A deep voice pounded through the bag.

Something landed on her jaw, and then another punch to her ribs made her buckle. They rolled her easily enough into the car.

Luce could kick herself for not being more proactive. She'd gotten lazy and left her gun in the center console of the SUV, her phone next to it. She hated being tied to technology, and now her tether was severed to anyone who could help.

"Christ."

"*Shut up. Boss said to do whatever it took to get you, so if you don't shut up, we shut you up.*" The heavy Russian accent left no question as to who had abducted her.

"You okay?" Maggie shook Luce's hand, her voice gentle.

Luce offered up a weak smile. "Yeah, I'm fine."

"I'd believe you if you didn't look like death warmed over."

"I'll be fine. I just need to get a shower, some bandages, and a note to my wife."

"Wife?"

"You know who I mean."

"I didn't know you two were that serious." Maggie kept her face concealed, looking out the window. They'd had a brief fling, but nothing noteworthy. If Luce didn't know better, she would have sworn she heard a hint of jealousy laced in those words.

Maggie and Luce were cut from the same button-down. Professionals, with high-power pressure, late nights, and too much energy that needed to be burnt off before going home. That's why they'd clicked that night at The Dungeon many years ago. Now, Maggie was showing Luce a side she hadn't seen in a long time.

She hoped it wouldn't be a problem. Besides, Maggie liked to drive stick as much as she liked being a vegetarian, and Luce's gate swung only one way. That was Brooke's way.

Chapter Twenty-six

Brooke waited for Sammy to say something. When he didn't offer anything, she stood and walked to the bar. "Want something?"

"No, thank you, Ms. Erickson." Sammy didn't look at Brooke as he said, "I have my men looking for the oyabun. They think they have a lead on an apartment Petrov uses for prostitution."

"You think Luce might be there?"

"I'm not sure. They saw Petrov leave and go to your house."

"My house? Why would he do that?"

Sammy shrugged.

"Are they still following him?"

"Yes, but he hasn't left your house yet."

"Why would he be there?"

"I don't know. I came as soon as I got the news."

Brooke scrubbed her face. What was Petrov up to? He was getting cocky if he thought he could walk the streets without being seen. But that didn't explain what he was doing at her place.

"How many men does he have with him?"

"One."

"One?"

"Yes, ma'am."

"I see."

"They're waiting outside."

"Maybe Luce is inside there?"

"I don't think so, Ms. Erickson."

"Why do you say that?"

"Someone heard a commotion in the apartment and saw men running out looking for someone."

"Luce?"

"All they could find out was that a few Russians were asking about someone."

"Luce."

Brooke rolled the tumbler between her hands, watching the liquid swirl up the sides. She sat down and took a sip. The bourbon burned her unanointed throat. Swallowing hard, she placed the glass on the table and looked at Sammy, whose expression was vacant. He was used to dealing with Luce, but she wasn't here, so he was going to have to deal with Brooke in her place.

"Send your men into the apartment, and let's see what they find."

Sammy pulled his phone and barked orders to his men.

They waited for a few moments before someone came back on the line.

"They said there's a dead man in the bathroom. Blood everywhere, but no Oyabun."

"That's good, right?"

Sammy shrugged.

"What else?"

"That's all I have."

"Tell them to get out of there. We'll call Colby and let her check it out."

Brooke was anxious. She needed a plan. This was Luce's territory. She always knew what to do. If Petrov was still at her place, then maybe he was looking for Luce, too.

"Tell your men to grab Petrov."

"Ma'am?"

Brooke shrugged. "He's at my house, probably on Luce's tail."

"But—"

Brooke picked up the tumbler and took another swallow. "If he puts up a fight, wound him."

"Wound him?"

"Why are you parroting everything I say?" Brooke took another swallow to bolster her courage. "Grab him, now. Take him somewhere no one can find him."

"Yes, ma'am."

"What about Frank?" Brooke asked.

"I'll handle him."

"Did you discover anything about Mei's family?"

Brooke knew she was putting a lot on Sammy's plate, but she didn't have time to worry about the workload. She needed to locate Luce and put all the players in play, if her plan was going to work.

"I have someone working on it in Japan."

"Who? Someone you can trust?"

"My brother."

"Oh. I didn't know you had a brother. I'm sorry."

Sammy bowed his head. "No apology necessary, Ms. Erickson. The oyabun has been very generous with my family. It is the least I can do to help."

"Thank you, Sammy."

"Ms. Erickson."

"Yes, Sammy."

"If I may offer some advice," he said, looking down at the floor.

"Of course."

"The job of an oyabun comes with heavy responsibilities. If she is not able to—"

"Don't say it, Sammy. Don't even think it." Brooke raised her hand. She wouldn't listen to the what-ifs or the what-might-happen crap. Luce was a survivor, and she would do whatever it took to save herself. She had to.

"I'm just saying that, if you make the decisions I think you want to make, it would be difficult for the men. The oyabun is, well, she is the boss."

"I understand what you're saying, Sammy. I appreciate the advice, but Luce isn't here to take care of things, so we must act in her place. Otherwise the opportunities to get Petrov and Frank will be gone."

"I understand, but—"

"We'll do our best to keep them alive and well until Luce returns. Revenge is for her to exact."

"Exactly," Sammy said, bowing.

"Fine. Since we are in agreement, perhaps we can focus on finding Frank, please."

"Of course, Ms. Erickson."

Brooke threw back the rest of the drink and slammed the glass on the table. She wasn't sure she was completely on board with Sammy, but she wasn't about to let him know that. If Luce died, Brooke wouldn't be responsible for her actions, and she knew Luce wouldn't stop her if it came to Luce's life or his.

"Revenge isn't always as cut and dried as you think, Sammy."

Chapter Twenty-seven

The warehouse was exactly like it had been just a few weeks ago, when Brooke was here last time. But this time, she wasn't wounded, Petrov didn't have her dangling as bait, and Luce wasn't risking her life. She could hear someone huffing in the darkness. In an odd way, she was taking perverse pleasure in this reveal. Her footsteps echoed in the dank interior. She could see Frank sitting under a single light suspended by bare wires. The scene was right out of a mobster movie. The only thing missing was a white polyester suit and a "little friend."

Brooke knew she was staring at the face of evil. He didn't flinch, he didn't move. In fact, he didn't even look at Brooke. Frank kept his eyes straight ahead. He didn't even blink. His back was straight, his wrists belted to the arms of the chair, his lips in a firm line. He looked like he'd lost weight since their last encounter, but not enough that Brooke would give him any sympathy. His bulk was still sizeable, and Brooke was smart enough to cut him a wide-enough berth that she was out of arm's reach. She fingered the gun in her jacket pocket. It would even the playing field.

Suddenly, all Brooke could see was Lynn lying in a pool of blood on her kitchen floor, vacant eyes staring straight ahead. Her mind grew cluttered with snapshots—images of Lynn, Frank, the knife she'd thrust into his thigh, the gun pointed at her face, and her hand covered in her own blood as he shot her. Instinctively, she rubbed her jaw, the pain intensifying as she stepped out of the shadows and closer to Frank.

"Aw, the oyabun's whore." Frank sneered, still not looking at Brooke.

Sammy stepped closer and raised his hand.

"Don't," Brooke commanded. "He's a defeated man, Sammy. He just doesn't know it, yet."

"Oh, have you found Luce?" Frank looked at her and laughed. "I didn't think so. She wouldn't let that little bitch do her dirty work for her." He nodded at Sammy.

"No, but she might let me," Brooke said.

"Ha-ha. Now that's funny."

"Is it?" Brooke looked around at the empty warehouse and registered the musty smell, mixed with grease and oil. She now knew why Luce kept the decrepit building. It was a good outpost for meting out a little attitude adjustment.

"You know what's funny, Frank? How you thought you could come back here and not get caught. Were you hanging around to see what Luce would do with Mei?"

"Ah, Mei. She is the spitting image of her sister, isn't she? Lucky find."

"Well, she isn't your daughter, that's for sure," Brooke said as she walked around Frank. "You could never produce something that innocent."

"Fuck you."

"We've played this game before, Frank. What I want to find out is how did you know JP had another daughter?"

He looked at Brooke and then at Sammy. He spit in Sammy's direction. He knew he was going to pay for the disrespect. He had to.

"How, Frank?"

"JP couldn't keep it in his pants. I'd cleaned up more than one mess for that bastard. I wouldn't be surprised if a few more little JPs aren't running around," he said, looking back at Brooke.

Clear disdain for Brooke radiated off Frank. He flexed his arms and pulled at the cuffs that were behind his back and laced through the metal chair.

"Why Mei?"

Frank didn't say anything, but his features softened for the briefest of moments. Something about Mei touched that stone-cold heart.

"You know Luce isn't going to let you live, right?"

He still sat motionless, but Frank's jaw worked overtime as he ground his teeth.

"What attitude do you think Mei will have toward you when she finds out you really aren't her father? You know she's going to know as soon as we bring her mother here."

Frank's neck practically snapped as he jerked around and scowled at Brooke. "Her mother is a whore just like you." He sneered.

Aw, she'd hit a nerve. She pressed on, going with her gut. "So, let me guess. You were involved with Mei's mother, weren't you?"

Brooke looked at Sammy, who couldn't hide the surprise on his face quick enough, and then suddenly his signature stoic expression was firmly back in place. She watched him step back and pull his phone. He was probably giving directions to his brother in Japan on the newest revelation.

Without stopping to think, Brooke reached down and grabbed Frank's leg. He grunted as she dug her thumb into the knife wound and squeezed. Small consolation compared to what he'd done to her.

Sammy ran to her side and grabbed Brooke's shoulder. Shaking him off, she shot him a look that told him they'd have words later. Brooke squeezed again, this time digging her fingernails into Frank's thigh.

He flexed his thigh out of Brooke's grasp and stomped his foot. "I'm going to kill you, bitch."

They were eye to eye, but Brooke didn't flinch. "You should have finished what you started, 'cause only one of us is going to make it out of this warehouse alive."

"You have no idea who you're messing with." Frank spit in her face as he spewed his words.

"Yes, I think I do, but you underestimated your position. You thought Petrov kidnapping Luce and Mei coming here to deliver your message would put her off her game. The only problem with that thinking is, you assume if you cut the head off the snake, it dies. A hydra has many heads, and just because Luce isn't here doesn't mean you aren't going to pay for what you've done."

"I bet you rehearsed that speech all the way here, didn't you?"

Brooke leaned back and smiled. Her hand on the gun suddenly felt like a good alternative to listening to his bullshit.

"Ms. Erickson, may I have a word?"

"Brooke stepped back, keeping her eyes on Frank. "What?"

"Petrov is on lock-down."

"Good. We'll let Luce handle him when she gets back."

"But—"

Brooke rolled her eyes at Sammy and stared him down. "I'm not done with Frank, yet. Don't get in the way, Sammy."

Sammy stiffened. "Ms. Erickson, my job is to protect you with my life. I'm not about to let you put yourself in danger."

"I'm not in danger, Sammy."

"You don't know Frank."

Brooke lifted her sweater, exposing her bullet wound. "I do know Frank. I saw Frank shoot Lynn. I saw Lynn lying in her own blood. Every night I close my eyes and see Lynn, her eyes are wide open staring back at me. I fucking know what Frank is capable of. Do you?"

"My apologies," Sammy said.

"You don't know what I'm capable of, Sammy."

"That's it. Give that little bitch a tongue-lashing. It is what you're good at, isn't it?" Frank said, looking at Brooke.

She wanted to slap that grin right off his face, but she wasn't about to let Frank get under her skin.

Brooke walked to Frank, pulled her gun, and pressed it against his temple. "No, you should be worried about me getting under your skin. You see, Luce isn't here to stop me, and I don't have to worry about family code, honor, or anything that might give you the opportunity to have an honorable death. You see, as I understand it, in your code, if you're going to die, it must be in an honorable manner." Brooke walked around Frank, dragging the muzzle around the crown of his head. "If I kill you, there wouldn't be any honor in it. Is that right, Sammy?"

"Yes, Ms. Erickson."

"Shut up, you little bitch," Frank said.

"Aw. Now see. Who's under whose skin now?"

Brooke felt a sudden sense of power. She could envision the bullet piercing Frank's skull, his head slumping forward and her nightmares ending. If only it were that easy.

"You're a whore. Luce's whore. When she's done with you, she'll have a new one to warm her bed. I hear Kat was crawling all over her at the club a couple of nights ago." Frank smiled. "A tomcat can't change how it strolls at night. It just does what's natural—fuck everything in sight."

Without stopping to think, Brooke backhanded Frank with the barrel of the gun. His cheek split, and blood oozed down his face. She stepped back and wanted to scream, but he was still smiling, knowing he'd won this time. Well, he'd paid for that little indiscretion.

Cockily, Frank turned toward Brooke and smiled. "You know I'm right. Ain't I right, Sammy?"

"Sammy, did you bring what I requested?" Brooke asked.

Sammy didn't say anything. He only bowed and left the room. Within a few minutes, he returned carrying a wooden box. Frank's expression fell as he recognized what was coming next.

"What, no arrogant statements now, Frank?" Brooke took the box from Sammy. "Bring that table over here," she instructed.

Chapter Twenty-eight

"Hey, sleepyhead. We're here." Maggie shook Luce.

Maggie was parked in her spot in the back of the club, but they were still outside. Luce didn't want to chance anything, so she stayed hidden.

"Get Gary, please."

Gary was a bouncer at The Dungeon and could bench-press a Chevy if he wanted to, which was most nights at the club.

"Why? What's wrong?"

"I think my foot's broken, and I couldn't move if I wanted to."

"Shit, Luce. I should just take you to the hospital." Maggie put the car in reverse and started to back out.

"No." Luce put her hand on Maggie's and stopped her. "They'll be looking for me everywhere, and they know how badly I'm beaten up. Just get Gary."

Maggie started to get out of the car, and Luce stopped her again. "Call him out here, please."

"Okay, right."

Luce knew she sounded paranoid, but she'd let her guard down lately, and she didn't intend to ever do that again. Petrov was a bigger bastard than she'd anticipated, and Luce had realized this even more fully after he'd almost killed Brooke, so she wouldn't put anything past him. Besides, he was at Brooke's apartment, and God only knew where else he'd invaded.

A quick call and Gary was standing on the driver's side of the car.

"What's up, Boss?"

"Can you help Luce out?"

"Sure thing."

Luce lifted the back of her seat and opened the door.

"Hey, Luce. Long time no see."

"Gary."

Without so much as a grunt, Gary popped Luce up out of the car and swung her into his arms. "You losing weight?"

"Naw. You're probably just getting stronger."

"Hmm." That was the most they'd talked to each other in years. Gary was small on talk and big on action, so he let his muscle do the speaking when it came to a customer seeing things his way. "Where you want her, Boss?"

"My room, Gary. Thank you."

The long, dark hallways were heaven to Luce's eyes. She'd found comfort in The Dungeon many a night before Brooke, and now it was her refuge once again.

Gary started to set Luce on a chair in the bedroom, but Maggie said something. "Put her on the bed, Gary. Can you get the first-aid kit from my office and make sure the doors are locked and everyone's gone? We're closing for the night."

Maggie had top-of-the-line first-aid kits. In the bondage business, you needed to be able to handle all matter of injuries, cuts, and bruises that would result from a black-hanky night. Gary brought the monstrosity and set it on the chair, nodded at Maggie and Luce, and finished his night's work. It would be daylight in a couple of hours, but many of the patrons of The Dungeon hung out late into the morning. Since it didn't open until ten p.m., late for some was almost six in the morning.

"You don't have to close on my account, Maggie."

"Don't worry. We only have a few stragglers anyway."

Luce pushed Maggie's hands away before she could even get started. "Maggie, please. Don't touch me. I need a shower to get three days' worth of scum off me. Do you have any feminine stuff?"

"You mean pads and—"

"Yep. Whatever you have will work until I get home."

"I'll start a bath, and then I'll find you something."

"Thanks."

In the empty room, Luce played out the last three days. She had no one to blame but herself. She'd let her guard down. Nabbing Marina Petrov had been a risky move, but she'd taken it without a second thought. She wanted Petrov to pay for his decision to make Frank a confidant and not giving him up the first time in the warehouse. Only she'd been the one to pay, three times. First Lynn, and then Brooke, and now herself.

God, how could she have been so stupid to not take precautions. She felt like she was lecturing her daughter for not having protection and ending up with a baby. No one was to blame but herself. Well, Luce wasn't one to dwell on the past. She'd moved forward, and Petrov was in her sights. He'd ultimately be rewarded for his mistakes, thrice.

Luce swung her legs off the bed and paid for the quick action. Her foot felt like it was about to fall off. Looking down at her boot, she realized she was going to regret the moment she had to get rid of it. It had kept the swelling down, but now she was going to have to peel it off and brace herself for the pain that would shoot through her.

"Fuck." She groaned as the blood rushed to the break. The foot was a beautiful purple, and now it didn't just throb. It sent a knife of pain slicing through her body.

"Fuck," she said for the second time in as many seconds. Swinging her foot back up onto the bed, she pushed a couple of pillows under it, raising it above her heart. That's what they said to do, right?

She clenched her jaw tight, grunting through the pain. She slowed her breath and took one, then two long, deep breaths. Focusing on the painting across from her, she meditated through the pain.

One, breathe.

Two, breathe.

Three, breathe.

Four, breathe.

Maggie busted through the door and broke Luce's concentration.

"Oh, shit. That looks bad, Luce."

Luce kept her eyes closed and focused on trying to reduce the agony coursing through her at the moment.

A mountain stream. The sound of rain as it moved around the rocks that tried to prevent it from going on its path. Water, fluid and moving. Nothing keeping it from reaching its goal of finding the larger pool. Merging with the greater pool. Soothing and fluid. Luce was water. Nothing would keep her from finding her path, her essence, as she moved to the great body of water.

Her grandfather stood before her, instructing her on the finer points of meditation. "Kaida, let your mind focus on nothing. Release the negative energy to the universe. Control your breathing. You are the master of all things surrounding you. Breathe," he said softly.

"Luce, you should have that looked at. It's really bad."

"Maggie, please."

Luce slowed her breathing, focusing on isolating the pain, but the moment was lost. The instant she released it, her foot throbbed uncontrollably.

"Your bath is ready, Luce. Do you want me to help you undress?"

"No. I'm good. Thanks, Maggie."

Luce felt as if she would be betraying Brooke if Maggie saw her naked, so she hobbled to the bathroom. Going through the pockets of the uniform, she placed her money, the gun, the watch, badge, and anything else she'd stuffed in there on the counter. Sitting on the side of the tub, she pushed the other boot off. After she opened the laces wide, she slowly eased it off her foot.

She sucked in a breath as the sudden rush of blood coursed through her foot. The pain was instantaneous. Gritting her teeth, she tried to hold in a groan and didn't move for several minutes, trying to breathe through the pain. Each time her heart beat her foot throbbed. Her mind throbbed, her body finally rebelling against the trauma of the last three days.

Swallowing hard, she stood and pushed her pants off and then shed her dirty underwear. She threw the bloody underwear, washrag, and bra on the floor in a pile. She'd have Maggie burn those items. She folded and stacked the security guard's black clothes. If she had time, she'd try to make sure he got all his stuff back, including his hat and other clothes, which she'd see got washed He'd been a lifesaver, and returning what few possessions he had was the least she could do.

Inspecting her body in the mirror was tough. She was battered and bruised everywhere. Bruises were turning magenta, dark purple, and beige, depending on whether they were new or older. Luce looked at her face. Whoever was looking back at her wasn't Luce. Brooke didn't need to see this person. She needed to see her wife. So that meant at least several days would have to pass before Luce would let Brooke see her. Sammy, though, was different. She needed to talk to him as soon as she could get word to him. Time was on her side now that she was free, but she didn't want to squander it, by any means.

As she lowered herself into the scented bubbles, the warm water enveloped her, welcoming her battered body. Her broken foot rested on the side of the tub, throbbing. The black-and-blue bruising was spreading out over the top and would probably get worse in the next few days. She wouldn't be walking anywhere, any time soon.

"Luce?"

"In here," Luce said, covering her face with the warm washcloth.

"I've got some ice for your face."

Maggie pulled the cloth off, and Luce saw her wince again. "Here. Put this on your eyes. It should help with the swelling. Everyone's gone."

"Thanks." The cold hurt bad enough that Luce tried to pull the ice pack off.

"Don't. You need to get the swelling down. If Brooke sees you like this, she's going to freak out."

"She isn't going to see me like this."

"Luce—"

"Maggie." Luce closed her eyes and reapplied the ice pack.

"I can send Gary out to get a message to Sammy."

"Do you have a burner?"

"Burner?"

"A cell phone you can get at any 7-11 or drugstore."

"No, but I can send Gary out to buy one."

"Okay. I've got some cash in my pants in that backpack." Luce pointed to the rucksack sitting with the clothes.

"I have money, Luce."

"I know, but so do I."

"Do you know Sammy's number?" Luce inquired.

She felt a headache starting at the back of her head and arching over the top toward her temples. A migraine. This night was never going to end, she thought, rubbing her temples.

Firm fingers pushed Luce's away and started to massage her head, running through her wet hair. Maggie's touch was oddly comforting. Luce relaxed into the touch.

"I had to guess at your number, so probably not. However, I can call my office in the morning and leave a message to him through Ms. Wentworth. She'll know how to get ahold of Sammy. Besides, I need some sleep before I talk to him. A few hours won't matter."

"Agreed."

Maggie picked up the washrag and rubbed it against Luce's neck and shoulders.

Stopping Maggie's hands, Luce said, "Maggie…"

"Relax. I know your heart belongs to someone else," she said, spreading soap on the rag and washing Luce's upper arm.

Luce would take the comfort Maggie was offering, but it would only go so far. She wouldn't give Brooke a reason to doubt their relationship. She'd pushed her away before, and that had been a disaster. Now all she wanted was to scrub the stench off her body, get some sleep, and reassess the situation in the morning when she had a clear head.

Everything would be better in the morning, Luce thought, letting herself drift off.

Chapter Twenty-nine

Luce woke with a start. Maggie was right. She should have eaten something with the pain pills. Without stopping to think, she swung her legs off the bed. The instant her foot hit the floor, she howled. Pain jagged up her leg and doubled Luce over.

"Christ." Pushing off the bed, Luce limped into the bathroom and fell to her knees just in time to chuck whatever was left in her stomach into the toilet. Her body jerked with each spasm as she expelled nothing but bile. Sitting back on her ass, she rolled over and hugged herself. A cold sweat was her reward for not following Maggie's instructions. She lay there for a moment, composing herself.

If Brooke were here, she'd have Luce's head coddled between her legs running her fingers through her hair, telling her everything was going to be all right. What she wouldn't give for that right now. A few more minutes—that's all she needed, just a little more time to pull herself together.

"Luce?" Maggie stormed through the bathroom door and knelt beside Luce. "What the hell happened?"

"Nothing. I'm good. I just thought the floor would be more comfortable than the bed."

"Luce. Did you eat the sandwich before you took those pain pills? Don't answer that," Maggie said, pulling Luce's head into her lap. Maggie ran her fingers through Luce's hair and rocked her back and forth. "You're as stubborn as an ox."

"One of my finer qualities, I assure you." Luce struggled to sit up. "Give me a hand, will ya?"

Luce wrestled with Maggie as she stood on one foot. Keeping as little weight as possible on the other, she nodded toward the sink. As she leaned against the edge, she ran her hands under the water and rinsed out her mouth.

"Blech," she said, spitting mouthfuls of water down the sink. "I think I need a drink."

"You don't need a drink. You need to rest and eat something." Maggie started to guide Luce toward the bed, then stopped. "Did you go to the bathroom?"

"Ah, no."

Luce shifted and moved back toward her first goal, relieving herself. "I don't need help with this part, Mags."

After turning her back, Maggie didn't move. "I'll just wait right here, and then it's back to bed with you." She looked over her shoulder at Luce. "I'm not taking no for an answer."

"Fine."

Luce dropped the lid and shuffled around Maggie, making her way toward the bed. "I need something for the pain, so can I just have a shot or two of bourbon?"

Maggie looked at her watch. "It's six in the morning, Luce. A little early, don't you think? Besides, you need a pain pill and more rest."

"You're starting to sound like a broken record, Mags." Luce reached for the phone on the bedside table. "Those things make me tired. Besides, I have a lot of work to catch up on."

"I'll make you a deal. You take a pain pill, eat something, and catch a catnap, and I'll call Ms.

Wentworth at the office and tell her to get a message to Sammy to meet me here at the club. I won't let you sleep past, say...eight."

"Maggie—"

"Look, Luce. I was your phone-a-friend last night, so take the doctor's advice and get some rest. Everything will still be here in two hours, and I'll have Sammy beside you waiting. Besides, what kind of friend would I be if I let you get killed out there?"

Luce was too tired to fight with Maggie. Truth be known, Maggie was right, and Luce was sure she wasn't thinking rationally. How could she? She'd had her ass kicked, and it was because of her own laziness.

"Fine, two hours, Maggie."

Maggie reached into her pocket and handed Luce another two pain pills and a glass of water.

Handing one back, she swallowed the pill with a gulp of water. "I only need one."

"Open," Maggie commanded her.

"What?"

"Open." Maggie motioned for Luce to open her mouth. "Good. It isn't that I don't trust you, but I know you, Luce. You have a one-track mind, and in your current situation, you'll get yourself killed. Now, eat this and I'll give Ms. Wentworth a call."

"Be careful of what you say, Maggie. Someone could be listening."

"I know." Maggie tucked Luce in and sat on the side of the bed. "Perhaps it would be better if I went down to the office and spoke with Ms. Wentworth personally. That way I could say I was looking for you, and she'll tell me you aren't around. I'll slip her a note, and we can get this ship righted."

"Hmm, yeah. That might work," Luce said, her

mouth full of sandwich.

"I help people hide things all the time, Luce. It's part of the bondage lifestyle. Secrets are my game, and I know how to keep them. Did I ever tell you about this congressman who came to the club? He had a particular fetish that if it got out could—"

Snores interrupted Maggie's story. "Well, fine. We'll just keep that for another day," she said, tucking the covers tighter around Luce. "He wasn't that good anyway. Total wuss."

Luce pulled the pillow tighter around her head and rolled to her side. Faking sleep was the only way she was going to get rid of Maggie, so she snored a little louder.

"Good night."

"Nite," Luce whispered.

Chapter Thirty

"Arrgh." Frank's scream echoed throughout the warehouse and pierced Brooke's ear. She leaned away, the tanto still embedded in the arm of the chair.

Brooke looked down, and Sammy's hand lay on top of hers. He'd helped her when she hesitated.

"Thank you," she whispered. Reaching down, she wrapped the pinkie in the white cloth it sat on and placed it in the small wooden box. "See that Frank gets that wrapped up."

"Of course, Ms. Erickson."

The men holding Frank looked at Brooke and bowed. She'd done something they all hoped they never had to do, offer a digit for an offense against the oyabun. They kept Frank still as Sammy wrapped his hand. It was more than Brooke would have offered, but their code was explicit, and they lived by a tight moral code. They would never disrespect the oyabun.

Brooke threaded her hands into Frank's hair and jerked his head back. "That was for Lynn. You should have paid with your life, but it isn't my revenge to exact. I'll take the pinkie as payment for what you did to me. I hope Luce is more magnanimous."

"Fuck you." He spat at Brooke.

Sammy slapped Frank across the face before Brooke could move.

"That record's getting old, don't you think?"

"Ha-ha-ha. You think you've got it all figured out. Luce is dead, and I'll be dancing on her grave soon enough." Frank stuck his tongue out and licked at the blood at the corner of his mouth.

"News flash. Petrov doesn't have Luce, but I have Petrov."

"You wish."

"Sammy." Brooke looked at Sammy and stuck her hand out.

He touched the face of the phone, lighting it up. After he touched it again, everyone could hear it ringing. He handed it to Brooke.

"Yeah, Sammy."

"This is Brooke. Put Petrov on the line, Sasha."

"Yes, ma'am."

"Fuck you. I'm not speaking to the phone. I'm going to kill every one of you sons-of-a-bitch." Petrov's voice boomed in the distance, but then they heard a slap—his reward for mouthing off.

"He doesn't want to come to the phone," Sasha said.

"Thanks. I believe we got what we needed." Brooke handed the phone back to Sammy.

He gave a few orders to Sasha and then ended the call. "Sasha will have him waiting when you're ready."

"Good. I'll call Colby and set up the handoff."

"I'm not sure about that, Ms. Erickson," Sammy said.

"We need to clear some of this off our plate, Sammy. We have Frank, and I think that will make her happy. Luce kidnapped Petrov's wife, so she could be brought up on kidnapping charges. As it is now, we have a man wanted for money-laundering, human trafficking, murder, and a host of other crimes that will put him away for decades."

Sammy shook his head, apparently still not convinced they were doing the right thing.

Brooke grabbed his arm and stopped him. "I'm the one who wanted this. You were only following orders, Sammy. You're damned if you do, and you're damned if you don't do what I say. I'll make sure Luce understands."

"Yes, ma'am."

"I'll call Agent Water and arrange the handoff."

"Yes, ma'am."

As Brooke pushed past Frank, she couldn't help but give him one last jab. "I hope Mei's reunion with her mother goes well. She'll need her when she finds out what a monster you are. Whatever JP was, at least he didn't steal someone else's child."

Frank's head bobbed up. "No. He just stole Luce's childhood by killing her mother. That's a demon she'll never shake, now will she?"

"Luce is much stronger than you'll ever know. I suspect you're going to find out just how strong. She doesn't have to resort to threats in the form of a tattoo on a person's body." Brooke leaned down and lifted his chin with a single finger. "How could you?"

"She would do anything for me. Ask her." Frank gave Brooke a leer that sickened her.

Brooke slapped Frank as hard as she could muster, jerking his head to the side. "You're an evil man. What kind of man would touch his daughter?"

"Like you said, she isn't my daughter."

Brooke shook with anger. Pulling her gun, she aimed it at Frank's head. "Then she won't miss you when you're gone."

Chapter Thirty-one

Something moved Luce's foot, stirring her awake. A man stood at the end of the bed with something in his hand.

"What the fuck?" She tried to pull her foot back, but he held her calf tight.

"Relax," Maggie said, walking out of the bathroom and handing him something. "He's putting a cast on your foot."

"Why?"

"Because it's clearly broken," the man said as he added another layer of wet plaster wrap. "I suspect from the bruising that you've broken more than one bone in the foot, probably at least three, and you need to stabilize it. Otherwise, it's not going to heal correctly, and you'll probably have problems walking if we don't set those bones."

"Luce, this is a personal friend, Dr. Tuck."

"Is that a joke?" Luce winced as she tried to flex her foot.

"Don't do that. You need to let this harden before you move it around." He shot Luce a cross look. "You're right, Maggie. She is a bad patient."

"See. That's why I called you over here. She wouldn't have made it to the office without me knocking her out."

"How did this happen?" He wrapped another layer around her foot and ankle.

"I fell."

"Hmm."

"Maggie, can I have a word with you?" Luce wiggled her finger at Maggie.

"As soon as the doctor's gone, sweetie."

Luce didn't want to make a scene in front of the man, and she didn't want to seem ungrateful for the personal service, but this needed to be kept private.

"I can assure you, my lips are sealed, Ms. Potter. I know who you are and of your reputation. I've seen some of your handiwork recently."

"What's that supposed to mean?" Luce pulled herself from his grasp and leaned back on the headboard.

"Let's just say I've repaired a few broken bones lately."

"Luce, relax. He's…well, he's familiar with the club and caters to a few well-known clients." Maggie winked at Luce.

"I haven't broken any bones here," Luce said defiantly.

"Ms. Water is a client of mine, Ms. Potter."

"Oh." Luce remembered the beating she'd given the DOJ agent.

"Yes, well, there you go. Don't walk on it for a few hours. I've brought a set of crutches, so you can get around. You can put some weight on it in a few days. Then I want you to come see me and let's check on how it's doing."

"Sure." Luce didn't intend to see the doctor again. In a few days, when it felt better, she'd cut the damn thing off herself.

"I'll make sure she comes by, Dr. Tuck. Thank you again for making a personal call."

Luce noticed Tuck clasp Maggie's hand and kiss the back of it as he walked out of the room.

"Oh, brother," she whispered.

Luce grabbed the crutches leaning against the bed and stood, trying to balance on one foot. Shoving them under her armpits, she tiptoed into the bathroom. She'd need to adjust them if she was even going to use the stupid things.

"Are you kidding me?" She guided herself onto the toilet and peered down at the flashing neon-pink cast. "Maggie," Luce screamed.

"What?"

"Did you tell him to do this?" She pointed to the cast.

"I think it's cute." Maggie chuckled.

"I don't. Get this thing off me." Luce reached down and tried to pry it off.

Maggie knelt and pulled Luce's hand away. "Stop, Luce. You have several broken bones in your foot, and from what Dr. Tuck said, it could be more than three. That was just a guess on his part without X-rays. Now if you want to limp like a dime-store cowboy the rest of your life, feel free to take it off."

Luce could hear Maggie talking to herself as she huffed out of the room. "No-good, ungrateful—"

"I can still hear you."

"Good."

Maggie slammed the door behind her.

"Aw, shit. Maggie," Luce yelled. She didn't want to seem ungrateful. Hell, she just wasn't good company right now. She had other things on her mind, like killing Petrov and Frank. Before she got up, Luce readjusted the crutches, then maneuvered them under her armpits to stand. Wobbling to the sink, she washed her hands and grabbed the washrag to clean her face.

As she stood in front of the mirror, she stopped. No wonder the doctor had looked at her the way he did. Her face was almost every color in an eight-pack of crayons. She'd gotten used to seeing things through swollen eyes, but looking at them now, it was a wonder she could see at all. Slits had replaced her normal almond-shaped eyes. Her cheeks were puffed up like she'd had the worst dental surgery possible, and her lips were split in several places. Her chin was tender to the touch and black, purple, and an odd shade of blue. It was a good thing he hadn't seen her before she'd cleaned up. The blood that leached into the tub drain made her worry that she'd sprung a leak beyond just her period.

Gently, she patted her face with the cold rag. Every inch of it hurt. Running her tongue around in her mouth, she could feel a few cuts, a loose tooth, but other than that, she felt lucky she didn't have a glass jaw. She didn't look forward to having it wired shut.

"When I get my hands on you, I'm going to kill you, Petrov. Trust me, this is nothing compared to what I'm going to do to you," she said in a threatening way to her reflection.

Luce leaned against the sink for support, her legs suddenly ready to give out on her. She felt like a newborn lamb, legs wobbly, head bobbing back and forth. She needed to lie down and quick. On impulse, she hopped on one foot and barely made it to the bed before the dizziness got her.

"Jesus."

The room spun as if she were smack-dab in the middle of the worst hangover she'd ever had. Turning over, she grabbed her head and moaned. She was going to make payback her bitch and spread it all over the guys who did this to her. At least Ivan was dead. He was one less person to worry about.

Crawling up the bed, she grabbed a pillow and hugged it tight. She jerked the covers over herself, rolled into a fetal position, and rocked back and forth. As a child, it had been the only way, when she was afraid, to comfort herself. Often times it was the nightmare of seeing her mother dead that woke her. She had called out in fear one night, but her father had answered her cries with the back of his hand, telling her to grow up, there was no such thing as monsters, that her mother was dead so get over it.

The pleasure she took when she killed him had been almost orgasmic. Every nightmare, every whipping, everything he'd done to her had culminated in those few precious moments. Even then, he'd taunted her, telling her she didn't have the guts. Well, Luce had finally proved him wrong, and he'd paid with his life. Maybe the last laugh *was* his.

Mei had popped up out of nowhere, wearing tattoos that ended with his name at the bottom. So maybe, just maybe, Luce had taken for granted that killing him had ended that story line. Obviously not. Now she wondered if Mei had played a part in the last few days.

Luce grabbed the phone, looked at the clock. Eight a.m.

Someone would be in the office by now. Dialing the number, Luce waited. Her lifeline was close, she could feel it.

"Potter Enterprises."

"Ms. Wentworth?"

"Ms. Potter. Oh my god, where are you? How are you? We've been worried sick."

"Is Sammy around?"

"No. He hasn't come in yet. Would you like me to call him?"

"Yes. I want you to give him this number and have him call me immediately," Luce said, relief coursing through her body. She was finally going home.

Chapter Thirty-two

Brooke's hand shook with the weight of the gun. She should pull the trigger, but revenge wasn't hers to take. It was Luce's. Once Luce heard what she'd found out, it would only be more fuel for that fire.

"You don't have the guts to pull that trigger," he said, turning and looking down the barrel. "Do you?"

Sweat rolled between her shoulder blades and beaded on her upper lip. Her nerves were firing, and her mind was bent on revenge. She caressed the rough ridges of the hammer with her thumb, then felt them bite into her skin as she cocked the hammer. Before she could answer Frank's question, Sammy's phone rang.

"It's Potter Enterprises."

"What?"

Sammy turned the phone toward Brooke. Her heart raced. "Answer it."

"This is Sammy."

Brooke kept her gun trained on Frank, rubbing the muzzle against his oily forehead. It would be so easy to just shoot him. Mei would never need to know. Her reunion with her mother would be a mixed blessing. Words buzzed around her as she turned to look at Sammy. His expression was indifferent as he spoke to the person on the other end.

"Ms. Erickson is here. I will share the message. Do you have a number? Thank you." Sammy pocketed the phone and shot a sideways glance at Brooke. "Luce is alive."

"Christ." Relief flooded her. Dropping the gun to her hip, she asked, "Where is she?"

❦❦❦❦

Luce examined her reflection in the mirror behind the bar in The Dungeon. She looked like she'd been beaten and left for dead. She still couldn't see out of her left eye, and the bruising was getting worse. She could have stuck a glacier on her face, but it wouldn't help the swelling go down. At least Brooke wouldn't be coming with Sammy. Maybe she could hide out for a few days before she saw her lover.

Luce sat there, rocking a glass of ice, the bourbon already evaporated. The face that looked back in the mirror behind the bar was grisly. Without thinking, she ran her fingertips over the bruises, wincing when she hit a tender spot. Unfortunately, every spot on it was tender to the touch. She let her tongue make a pass around her mouth, she was sure a visit to the dentist was in her future.

"Another one, mate?"

Luce nodded at Gary and jiggled her glass. "Yep."

Sammy had said he needed to drop something off, and then he'd be right over.

Luce held the glass against her face. Popping another painkiller, she winced internally. Mixing alcohol and pills wasn't a smart move, but she'd survived Petrov, so on the list of things that might kill her, this was at the bottom.

"You look like hell, Luce," Maggie said, her hand trailing over Luce's shoulder and down her arm.

Taking a seat next to her, Luce couldn't help but see the loving look in Maggie's gaze.

"Yeah. Well, I've been to hell, and trust me, this looks a lot better."

Luce rested her hand on the revolver—a keepsake for her growing collection.

"You know you don't need that, right?"

Luce shot Maggie a sideways glance. "Until I have my own gear, I do." She took another swig from her glass. "Hey, thanks for letting me crash here."

"Any time. You know that."

"Thanks, but let's not make a habit of you saving my ass."

Maggie just smiled and motioned for Gary to refill Luce's already-empty glass.

"So, here's the doctor's orders—stay off that foot for a couple of days. See your primary doctor, and make sure you ice that face." Maggie's fingers traced Luce's jawline, her intent obvious.

Before Luce could say anything, a familiar voice answered. "I'll make sure she follows the doctor's orders." Brooke's voice echoed down the hall as she approached them. Sammy stood next to Brooke, his discomfort clear as he avoided eye contact with Luce.

"Sammy, I told you not to bring Brooke."

"Did you think I'd let him leave me behind?" Brooke said, moving closer. "Besides, you scared the shit out of me, Luce Potter." Brooke turned Luce's face toward her for closer inspection.

"Jesus Christ." Colby Water moved from out of the shadow of the two.

"I see you've brought the cavalry," Luce quipped before swallowing the rest of her drink.

"I wanted to make sure we get you home in one

piece, lover." Brooke kissed Luce's cheek.

"Hello, Agent Water. I don't think we've been introduced," Maggie said, sticking her hand across the bar.

"Ma'am."

"Agent Water meet Dr. Maggie Williams. Maggie, Agent Water," Luce said blithely.

"Nice to meet you, Doctor." Colby gave a toothy grin.

Shit. Luce had seen Colby in various stages of her work persona, but she hadn't seen the cougar version until now.

"How's the patient?"

"Well, you can see for yourself."

"Geez, you sure do like living on the razor's edge, don't you, Potter?"

"Thank you for that assessment of my life, Agent Water. Now perhaps you can tell me what the hell you're doing here."

"I was invited."

Before Luce could say anything, Brooke's hands assessed every inch of Luce's body. Her overt manhandling in front of everyone was a little embarrassing, but Luce welcomed the feel of her lover's touch. Her lips touched Luce's ear. "Are you ready to go home?"

"In a minute—"

"Who did this to you, Potter?"

"I don't know," Luce lied. Pulling Brooke closer, she nuzzled Brooke's neck. God, she smelled good. "How are you? Shouldn't you be home resting?"

Brooke gently ran the tips of her fingers over Luce's face. "Did he do this to you?"

Luce wanted to say yes, but with Colby standing

there, she wasn't going to lose her chance at getting Petrov.

Gently, Brooke kissed her swollen eye and then her lips. "I'm sorry."

"Look, Potter. Let me tell you how this is going down. You're going to turn Petrov over to me—"

"I don't have him."

"No, but she does," Colby said, pointing to Brooke.

"What? How?"

"I don't know how, but as I said, this is how it's going down. I take Petrov, and you're going to release his wife and daughter, or—"

"Wait. What?" Luce ping-ponged from Colby, to Brooke, to Sammy. Each, with the exception of Colby, avoided her gaze.

"Seems Brooke's been a busy little bee while you've been missing for the last couple of days."

Luce turned around in the bar stool, leaning back against the bar, which gave her a better view of her lover.

"Can I get one of those?" Colby sat in the stool next to Luce.

Gary looked at Maggie, who nodded and said, "Better make it another round for everyone. I want to hear this, too."

※※※※

Brooke gazed at Luce, wondering how she'd feel about the deal she'd made with Colby. She would do whatever it took to keep her lover safe. Now if only Luce would agree. She'd had Sammy take Frank someplace safe, but Luce didn't need to know that, yet. She'd told

Sammy to meet her at The Dungeon. The only way Brooke could put the rest of her plan into action and get Petrov out of their lives for good was if she called Colby to offer Petrov. Brooke had explained to Colby what she'd done and that Colby could have him on one condition: she'd have to be part of her plan. She suspected Colby wouldn't have any trouble playing bad cop and threatening to have Brooke arrested for kidnapping if Luce didn't concede. She crossed her fingers. Knowing Luce, she'd be suspicious of anything Colby said, but she actually wanted Petrov dead once and for all.

"It was my idea, Luce." She absently ran a finger over a vein in Luce's hand. "I thought you might go to my house, since I figured Petrov would be watching yours."

Brooke picked up the tumbler and took a sip, trying to buy her more time to get everything straight in her head. "So I put someone at the house, and sure enough he showed up."

"Stupid bastard," Luce said.

"As soon as the men called Sammy, I told them to grab him. I don't think he was expecting them to do that." Brooke smiled internally. She herself was surprised at how easy it had been to snatch the mobster.

"Just like that?" Luce looked at her.

"Just like that."

Sammy piped up. "Oyabun, I can explain."

"Well, someone better."

Everyone started to talk all at once.

"Stop." Luce slapped the bar.

Brooke jumped, and the tumbler she'd been holding fell to the ground with a crash. Looking at Maggie, she mouthed an apology. Maggie offered a smile and nodded to Gary, who sprang into action to clean up the mess.

"My painkillers are starting to wear off, and I just want some answers, now." Luce's voice boomed in the empty club.

The room fell silent.

"You better let Brooke explain, Potter," Colby said, looking at Sammy but pointing to Brooke.

"Brooke," Luce said, glancing at Sammy and then at her lover.

"I'm sorry, but I had to do something. We didn't know what had happened, where you were, but I knew Petrov had to be involved after we saw the video of your being kidnapped and I...well, I just had to do something."

"There was a ransom?"

"Ransom? No," Brooke said, confused by Luce's question.

"Well, you said there was a video, so I assume he sent it." Luce looked at Brooke, then Sammy, and finally rested her gaze on Colby, who returned a stern look. "What did you do, honey?" Luce finally looked at Brooke.

The cool tone gave Brooke pause. She held Luce as she explained how she'd come up with the plan to get Petrov and deal with the women.

"And?"

"I had Sammy bring the women back. I was prepared to trade them for you, if I had to."

"Hmm." Luce stared at Sammy, who didn't flinch as she eyed him.

Brooke continued. "I—"

"And you went along with this?"

"He didn't have a choice. I told him you'd fire

him for being disloyal if he didn't do what I said."

Everyone sat in silence, digesting the plan Brooke had concocted.

Colby piped up. "Look, Potter. I was getting ready to station my own men at the house on the off chance you'd go there. We'd have caught him if Brooke hadn't swooped in and beat us to it."

Brooke nuzzled closer and whispered, "I'll explain the rest in the car."

"So what's it going to be, Potter? Hand him over or have me arrest Brooke and you for kidnapping?" Colby was playing bad cop to the hilt. The only problem was they hadn't talked about charging Luce with kidnapping.

"Let's go home. I need to prop this thing up and think about everything."

Colby pressed the issue. "Hold on there, Potter. No one's leaving until you decide."

Brooke knew Colby was forcing Luce's hand, but she was taking it a little too far. Brooke was counting on the fact that Luce wouldn't want her to be arrested, but the push-back on Colby's part might be too much. Luce was a proud woman and wasn't one for coercion.

"You'll drop the charges against Brooke?"

"That's the deal."

Brooke broke in. "What about the charges against Luce?"

Colby snapped around and tossed Brooke a glare. Brooke stood at the challenge. They hadn't talked about charging Luce with anything, and she wasn't about to let Colby change their agreement.

"I know you wanted this to go down differently, Potter. However, it's best for everyone if you release those women. Petrov will go down for the murder of

Lynn, money laundering, and human trafficking—the whole shebang." Colby stood and patted Luce on the shoulder. "Try to stay out of my way, and you won't be charged with anything. ID him as your kidnapper, and I'll add that to the list of charges."

"I don't know who did this," Luce said, pointing down at her foot.

"And I suppose you don't know anything about a dead guy in the apartment."

"I have no idea what you're talking about."

Luce finished her drink and stood, leaning on Brooke.

"Have it your way. I'll be in touch," Colby said. Looking at Maggie, she said, "It was a pleasure to meet you, Doctor. Perhaps our paths will cross again." She offered Maggie a sly smile.

Ever the rogue, Brooke thought, watching the exchange.

"Oh…" Colby stopped and looked back at Luce. "I hear you have a long-lost sister. JP sure seemed to be a busy guy, huh? Anything I should know about that?"

"Family business. I'm sure you'll understand if I don't want to talk about it."

"Of course, but if I can help, let me know."

"Thanks, but I think I've got this handled."

"I'm sure you do. Well, as I said, I'll be in touch." Colby smiled at Brooke, then walked away.

Brooke waited until Colby was out of the club before she said anything else. "Ready to go home?"

"Yep, and I think you have some explaining to do, honey." Luce stumbled as she tried to take a few steps.

Sammy rushed to Luce's side and swung her arm over his shoulders. "I gotcha, Oyabun."

"Thanks, Maggie," Brooke said, offering her hand.

"I'll come by and check in on her later."

"Thanks."

All Brooke wanted to do was get Luce home and in bed. She'd tell Luce everything later, assuming Luce didn't grill her on the way home.

"You have a lot of explaining to do," Luce said, hobbling toward the door.

"You have no idea," Brooke said, rubbing her back.

Chapter Thirty-three

Luce settled onto the backseat of the SUV, leaning against Brooke. Her lover's perfume bathed her in sensory overload. It was comforting and reassured her this wasn't a dream. She wanted to purge herself of the events of the last few days, but these new developments required an explanation.

"You want to tell me what really happened?" Luce looked up at the rearview mirror, directing her question to her number one.

"Boss, I can explain."

"It's not his fault, Luce." Brooke came to Sammy's defense. "Are you mad at me?"

She didn't respond. Luce wanted to be pissed, but she couldn't muster up the energy. Part of her was relieved Petrov was going away for a long time, but part of her wanted to exact her own type of justice on him. He didn't deserve the leniency the court would afford him. Three squares and a cot were too good for that bastard. He'd find a way to run his operation from prison, and when he did, Luce would be waiting to throw a wrench in the operations. Her only hope was to find Frank and put a stop to his plans.

"Sammy, can you hand me that box?" Sammy passed the wooden box back to Brooke. "I know this won't make up for what I did," Brooke said, handing Luce the small offering.

"I can't be bought, my love," Luce said.

"I know, but just know I did this for us. I want Petrov behind us. I wanted him out of our lives, and I didn't know what else to do. I thought…" She started to cry. Luce pulled Brooke tighter against her, wincing as she squeezed Luce. "Sorry."

"It's fine. Now stop crying. I would have done the same thing."

Luce knew that was only half true. She would have killed Petrov slowly, agonizingly slowly.

Cradling the box in her hands, she looked at Brooke. "What's this?'

"Open it. Perhaps it'll make up for losing Petrov."

Luce slid the top back and stared at the bloody white wrapping. She didn't have to unwrap it. She knew what it was.

"Sammy? Show me your hand," Luce demanded. He raised his hand. "Show me the other."

"It isn't his, Luce."

"Show me yours," she ordered Brooke.

"It's not mine."

"Whose is it? Petrov's?"

There was a long moment of silence before Brooke said anything. "It's Frank's."

"What?"

"I told you I'd been busy."

Luce closed the box, more than shocked. She'd completely underestimated her lover. Looking down at the box, she could only shake her head. Brooke had a side to her that she'd love exploring further.

Epilogue

Luce had sat in the courtroom every day watching the judicial system play out their idea of justice. Colby Water had been the lead witness in his prosecution, and after Petrov was found guilty on all counts, sentencing was today. Only Luce had opted not to be in the courtroom for the reading. From her vantage point, she could see the transport van wedged between two buildings. The line of orange jumpsuits shuffled their way to the van, followed by Colby Water. She probably wanted to make sure the dirtbag got in the van without any issues.

How noble, Luce thought.

She spied Petrov dead center of the pack. His shit-eating grin was easy to spot as he said something to the prisoner behind him. Luce trained her sight on his head, just behind his ear, and slid her finger down to the trigger.

Suddenly, a commotion broke the line, and the group stumbled, most falling to the ground as they were dragged down when he fell.

"Get the fuck up," one of the deputies said as he rushed over to pick Petrov up. When Petrov didn't move, the deputy repeated his order and yanked Petrov's arm. Blood spread around Petrov's hand, coloring the orange jumpsuit a nasty shade of black.

Colby ran to his side, knelt, and pressed her hand against the wound. The guard stomped on the prisoner shackled behind Petrov, forcing the prisoner to drop the bloody, makeshift shank.

"Get a fucking ambulance, now," Colby yelled. Popping her head up, she looked around. "Shit, Potter."

Deputies pulled their weapons and took defensive positions around the chain gang.

"Now that's justice, Yakuza style," Luce said, watching the melee below. "Let's go, Sammy."

"Nice job, Oyabun." Sammy slapped her on the back.

She flashed the briefest of smiles. She wasn't one for emotional outbursts, but she had to agree that it was a nice job. She hadn't had to use the shooting skills she always kept up at the range. Her plan had kept her off the radar. The man who'd taken the job had nothing to lose. His life sentence had propelled him to contact Luce and offer his services, for a price. She could afford to take care of his family and protect them from Petrov's goons.

Luce broke down the gun and stowed it in the duffel.

"I'll take this, Oyabun," Sammy said, reaching for the case.

"Remember, justice isn't always found in the courtroom. Now, let's go take care of Frank."

About the author

Award winning, international best selling author, Isabella, lives in California with her wife and three sons. Isabella's first novel, Always Faithful, won a GCLS award in the Traditional Contemporary Romance category in 2010. She was also a finalist in the International Book Awards, and an Honorable Mention in the 2010 and 2012 Rainbow Awards.

She is a member of the Rainbow Romance Writers, Romance Writers of America and the Golden Crown Literary Society. She has written several short stories and just finished her next novel, Aphrodite's Handmaiden. She is current working on Cigar Barons. A family saga where - bloood isn't thick than water, when it comes to a family dynasty. It's due out late 2017

Other Isabella titles available at Sapphire Books

Award winning novel - Always Faithful
ISBN - 978-0-9828608-0-9

Major Nichol "Nic" Caldwell is the only survivor of her helicopter crash in Iraq. She is left alone to wonder why she and she alone. Survivor's guilt has nothing on the young Major as she is forced to deal with the scars, both physical and mental, left from her ordeal overseas. Before the accident, she couldn't think of doing anything else in her life.

Claire Monroe is your average military wife, with a loving husband and a little girl. She is used to the time apart from her husband. In fact, it was one of the reasons she married him. Then, one day, her life is turned upside down when she gets a visit from the Marine Corps.

Can these two women come to terms with the past and finally find happiness, or will their shared sense of honor keep them apart?

Forever Faithful
ISBN - 978-1-939062-75-8

Life is what happens when you make other plans, and Nic and Claire have just found out that life and the Marine Corps have other plans for their lives.

Nic Caldwell has served her country, met the woman of her dreams, and has reached the rank of Lieutenant

Colonel. She's studying at one of the nation's most prestigious military universities, setting her sights on a research position after graduation. Things couldn't be better and then it happens; a sudden assignment to Afghanistan derails any thoughts of marriage and wedded bliss. Another combat zone, another tragedy, and Nic suddenly finds herself fighting for her life.

Claire Monroe loves her new life in Monterey. She's finally where she wants to be, getting ready to start her master's program at the local university, watching her daughter, Grace, growing up, and getting ready to marry the love of her life. What could possibly derail a perfect life? The Marine Corps.

Will Nic survive Afghanistan? Can Claire step up and be the strength in their relationship? Or will this overseas assignment and a catastrophic accident divide their once happy home?

Broken Shield
ISBN - 978-0-9828608-2-3

Tyler Jackson, former paramedic now firefighter, has seen her share of death up close. The death of her wife caused Tyler to rethink her career choices, but the death of her mother two weeks later cemented her return to the ranks of firefighter. Her path of self-destruction and womanizing is just a front to hide the heartbreak and devastation she lives with every day. Tyler's given up on finding love and having the family she's always wanted. When tragedy strikes her life for a second time she finds something she thought she lost.

Ashley Henderson loves her job. Ignoring her mother's advice, she opts for a career in law enforcement. But, Ashley hides a secret that soon turns her life upside down. Shame, guilt and fear keep Ashley from venturing forward and finding the love she so desperately craves. Her life comes crashing down around her in one swift moment forcing her to come clean about her secrets and her life.

Can two women thrust together by one traumatic event survive and find love together, or will their past force them apart?

American Yakuza
ISBN - 978-0-9828608-3-0

Luce Potter straddles three cultures as she strives to live with the ideals of family, honor, and duty. When her grandfather passes the family business to her, Luce finds out that power, responsibility and justice come with a price. Is it a price she's willing to die for?

Brooke Erickson lives the fast-paced life of an investigative journalist living on the edge until it all comes crashing down around her one night in Europe. Stateside, Brooke learns to deal with a new reality when she goes to work at a financial magazine and finds out things aren't always as they seem.

Can two women find enough common ground for love or will their two different worlds and cultures keep them apart?

Executive Disclosure
ISBN - 978-0-9828608-3-0

When a life is threatened, it takes a special breed of person to step in front of a bullet. Chad Morgan's job has put her life on the line more times that she can count. Getting close to the client is expected; getting too close could be deadly for Chad.

Reagan Reynolds wants the top job at Reynolds Holdings and knows how to play the game like "the boys". She's not above using her beauty and body as currency to get what she wants. Shocked to find out someone wants her dead, Reagan isn't thrilled at the prospect of needing protection as she tries to convince the board she's the right woman for a man's job. How far will a killer go to get what they want? Secrets and deception twist the rules of the game as a killer closes in.

How far will Chad go to protect her beautiful, but challenging client?

American Yakuza II - The Lies that Bind
ISBN - 978-10939062-20-8

Luce Potter runs her life and her business with an iron fist and complete control until lies and deception unravel her world. The shadow of betrayal consumes Luce, threatening to destroy the most precious thing in her life, Brooke Erickson.

Brooke Erickson finds herself on the outside of Luce's life looking in. As events spiral out of control Brooke can only watch as the woman she loves pushes her further away. Suddenly, devastated and alone, Brooke refuses to let go without an explanation.

Colby Water, a federal agent investigating the ever-elusive Luce Potter, discovers someone from her past is front and center in her investigation of the Yakuza crime leader. Before she can put the crime boss in prison, she must confront the ultimate deception in her professional life.

When worlds collide, betrayal, dishonor and death are inevitable. Can Luce and Brooke survive the explosion?

Surviving Reagan
ISBN - 978-1-939062-38-3

Chad Morgan has finally worked through the betrayal of her former client and lover, Reagan Reynolds. Putting the pieces of her life back in order, she finds herself on a collision course with that past when she takes on a new client, the future first lady. Unfortunately, Chad's newest job puts her in the cross-hairs of a domestic terrorist determined to release a virus that could kill thousands of women.

Reagan Reynolds has paid for her sins and is ready to start a new life. Attending a business conference in Abu Dhabi gives her the opportunity to prove to her father and herself that she's worthy of a fresh start. Her past will intersect with her future at the conference when she accidentally comes face-to-face with Chad Morgan.

Time is running out. Will Reagan confront Chad? Can she convince Chad she's changed, or will death part them forever?

Writing as Jett Abbott

Scarlet Masquerade
ISBN - 978-0-982860-81-6

What do you say to the woman you thought died over a century ago? Will time heal all wounds or does it just allow them to fester and grow? A.J. Locke has lived over two centuries and works like a demon, both figuratively and literally. As the owner of a successful pharmaceutical company that specializes in blood research, she has changed the way she can live her life. Wanting for nothing, she has smartly compartmentalized her life so that when she needs to, she can pick up and start all over again, which happens every twenty years or so. Love is not an emotion A.J. spends much time on. Since losing the love of her life to the plague one hundred fifty years ago, she vowed to never travel down that road again. That isn't to say she doesn't have women when she wants them, she just wants them on her terms and that doesn't involve a long term commitment.

A.J.'s cool veneer is peeled back when she sees the love of her life in a lesbian bar, in the same town, in the same day and time in which she lives. Is her mind playing tricks on her? If not, how did Clarissa survive the plague when she had made A.J. promise never to change her?

Clarissa Graham is a university professor who has lived an obscure life teaching English literature. She has made it a point to stay off the radar and never become involved with anything that resembles her past life. Every once in a while Clarissa has an itch that needs to be scratched, so she finds an out of the way location to scratch it. She keeps her personal life separate from her professional one, and in doing so she is able to keep her secrets to herself. Suddenly, her life is turned upside down when someone tries to kill her. She finds herself in the middle of an assassination plot with no idea who wants her dead

Scarlet Assassin
ISBN 978-1-939062-36-9

Selene Hightower is a killer for hire. A vampire who walks in both the light and the darkness, but lately darkness has a stronger pull. Her unfinished business could cost her the ability to live in the light, throwing her permanently back into the black ink of evil.

Doctor Francesca Swartz led a boring life filled with test tubes, blood trials, and work. One exploratory night, in a world of leather and torture, she is intrigued by a dark and solitary soul. She surrenders to temptation and the desire to experience something new, only to discover that it might alter her life forever.

Will Selene allow the light to win over the darkness threatening the edges of her life? Two women wonder if they can co-exist despite vast differences, as worlds collide and threaten to destroy any hope of happiness. Who will win?

CPSIA information can be obtained
at www.ICGtesting.com
Printed in the USA
FSOW01n1741030217
30261FS